CHRISTMAS *at the*
NANTUCKET
RESTAURANT

CHRISTMAS *at the* NANTUCKET RESTAURANT

A NOVEL

PAMELA KELLEY

sourcebooks landmark

Published by Sourcebooks Landmark, an imprint of Sourcebooks
1935 Brookdale RD, Naperville, IL 60563-2773
(630) 961-3900
sourcebooks.com

Previously self-published as *Christmas at the Restaurant* in 2020.

Cataloging-in-Publication Data is on file with the Library of Congress.

Printed and bound in the United States of America.
VP 10 9 8 7 6 5 4 3 2 1

1

Mandy Lawson stood in the dark and stared out the kitchen window while she waited for the water to heat for her tea. It was late, almost ten, and the normally gorgeous view of Nantucket Sound was shrouded in darkness. But in the distance, she saw a pinprick of light. Probably a boat bobbing on the water, growing brighter as it drew closer to shore. She watched it for a moment, then turned on the light, took her favorite caramel-flavored herbal tea out of the cupboard, popped it in a mug, and added the hot water.

The kids were finally in bed. They had stayed

up later than usual, excited about the holidays and a party at school the next day. Mandy had made cupcakes earlier for Brooke to bring in. Normally, Mandy looked forward to this time of year. The magic and wonder of Christmas through the eyes of her children never failed to lift her spirits. This year was a little different though. It felt off, a bit empty. Last year at this time, she was newly separated from her husband, and it was all a blur. Now, she was officially divorced and in recent months had started dating someone. She enjoyed his company, but it wasn't terribly serious yet and the holidays had a way of magnifying everything.

Thinking back to happier days with Cory and the kids also made her reflective and a bit sad. Cory had moved on. He wasn't dating anyone seriously as far as she knew, but he was dating, a lot—which he'd apparently also been doing during the final years of their marriage. The kids seemed to be doing fine too. She had to give Cory credit. He was very good with them. He lived close enough that he took them regularly, and they were able to fill in for each other as needed. Mandy just missed how things used to be. The house often felt too big for the three of them without Cory there. But it was the house the kids had grown up in, and she didn't want to uproot them. She knew stability was important.

She took her tea bag out of the mug and tossed it in the trash, then headed to the family room to settle into her favorite armchair, put her feet up, and read for a while before bed. She wasn't sleepy yet. It had been a busy day at the restaurant. She co-owned Mimi's Place with her sisters, Emma and Jill, and Paul, the chef. She smiled, thinking of how clever their grandmother had been, leaving it to them in her will with the stipulation that they had to work together for a year before making any major decision to sell.

Jill was a silent partner, having returned to Manhattan after the year was up to continue running the search firm she owned with her partner,

Billy, who was now her husband. But it had been exactly what both Emma and Mandy needed. Emma's marriage had imploded as well, but in a very different way when her husband of many years left her for another man. Emma and Paul Taylor, the chef at Mimi's Place, had been childhood sweethearts, and Mandy was glad that they had grown close again, once Emma was ready to let someone in.

For Mandy, Mimi's Place had been a godsend. She'd been wanting to go back to work for years, but Cory had discouraged it. They hadn't needed the money. He ran a successful hedge fund that generated millions in income each year, and he liked being able to brag about his wife not needing to work. But she had needed it. She needed to feel useful and challenged. And she found that with the restaurant.

Emma had some experience working as a waitress during college. And Jill had tended bar. Mandy had the least experience of the three, never having worked in a restaurant, but she had set up many local charity events. That experience turned out to be invaluable as they expanded the business into doing more weddings and other functions.

Mandy settled into her comfy baby-blue chair, which was covered in a soft plush velour. She glanced at her book waiting for her on the side table, but she was feeling a little too tired to read and decided to see what was on the Hallmark Channel instead. The Christmas movies always put her in a good mood. She'd just picked up the remote and clicked on the TV when she heard a soft giggle, followed by a hiccup and then another giggle, slightly louder this time.

She smiled as she glanced at the huge decorated Christmas tree that stood a few feet away from the big-screen television. It was in the corner, and the sounds of two giggling children came from behind it. They must have stealthily crept back downstairs while she was in the kitchen and hidden in their favorite spot. She stood up and could see two pairs of feet peeking out from where Blake and Brooke were lying down with their heads close together, looking up at the tree.

Mandy knew it was special back there. She'd once shared with them that she and her sisters used to crawl behind their Christmas tree and stay there for hours, gazing at the twinkling lights, drinking in the Christmas spirit, and dreaming about their futures. It was a magical feeling, and she was glad they were experiencing it. But it was still way past their bedtime.

"I can see and hear both of you. Come out now and get back to bed. It's very late."

There was a moment of silence and then shuffling as they wiggled their way out.

"Mom, it's so cool back there. You have no idea!" Blake said excitedly.

"Actually, I do, honey. Go on up to bed. You'll have plenty of time to hang out behind the tree over the next month."

Mandy followed them upstairs and made sure

they were both tucked securely in bed before heading back downstairs. She'd just settled back in her chair when her cell phone rang. It was her sister Jill.

"Perfect timing. I just put the kids to bed."

They chatted for a few minutes, catching up on things, and then Jill was quiet for a moment. It was a bit unusual for her to call so late. They usually talked in the morning.

"Is everything okay?" Mandy asked.

"Yes! Everything is fine. Billy and I were just talking and… Well, I remembered you said we were welcome to stay with you anytime and that you had plenty of room with Cory gone."

"Yes. Did you two want to come for the Nantucket Stroll?" They'd talked about it ages ago. The first weekend in December was the famous Nantucket Christmas Stroll, when all the stores were decorated for the holidays and restaurants reopened or stayed open through the weekend for a final hurrah before closing for the winter.

"Yes. We'd love to come over Thursday afternoon, if that works."

"Of course. We could use your help at the restaurant too. It should be a busy weekend."

"Good. It will be fun to get behind the bar again. Billy says he's happy to help too." Mandy thought about that for a moment. Billy Carmenetti was tall, dark-haired, and very charming. The customers would love him.

"Maybe we'll have him help at the front desk, greeting people and making them feel welcome."

Jill laughed. "That's perfect. If it's okay with you, we'd like to stay for a few weeks. Through New Year's Eve, if that's not too much. If it is, we can head to the White Elephant."

Mandy suddenly felt her mood lift even more. "Jill, I would love that. It would be great to have you here all month. Truth be told, I could use the company. It's been a little hard this time of year."

"I wondered if it might be. We will totally cheer you up. We'll do all the holiday things—baking, eating, Christmas shopping, and just relaxing and enjoying some good wine. I can't wait to catch up with you and Emma, and Paul too. It's going to be a great Christmas."

They talked for almost an hour, until they both started yawning. Mandy hung up and headed upstairs to go to bed, feeling relaxed and, for the first time, looking forward to the weeks ahead.

Mandy dropped the kids off at school the next morning, and as she turned onto Main Street toward the restaurant, her phone rang. She smiled as she answered the call.

"Hi, Matt."

"Good morning." His rich, deep voice was one of the first things she'd noticed about him. He'd stopped smoking years ago, but there was still a slight rasp. "Did you by chance hear me out on the water last night? We were out late fishing and on our way in, we passed by, and I flashed my lights and tooted the horn. I didn't want to call you because it was late, around ten."

She laughed. "I did see a boat out there, but I didn't make the connection that it was you. How did you do?"

"Not a single bite, but I expected that. Fish are mostly gone. It was a fun time though. I hadn't seen Kevin in a while, so it was good to have a few beers and catch up. I'm checking in to see if we're still on for dinner tonight."

"Yes, definitely. Cory has the kids, and I'm looking forward to it." Mandy loved her children, but also valued her quiet time with Matt. They were both so busy that she only saw him once or twice a week.

"Great. I'll come by around seven, and we'll see what we're in the mood for. Maybe the Gaslight?" It was one of their favorite restaurants.

Mandy was still smiling as she ended the call and pulled up to Mimi's Place. Things were going well with Matt. They'd started dating recently. He'd been coming into the restaurant regularly with friends for dinner or even sometimes by himself after work and usually ate at the bar. They'd chatted often when it was slow, and Matt knew she was going through a divorce. While she'd sensed some interest from him many months ago, she'd also made it clear that she wasn't ready to date.

It wasn't until after her sister Jill's wedding in August that Mandy suddenly noticed Matt in a different way. And she finally felt ready. So different from her ex-husband, Cory, who never had a stretch where he wasn't dating. Even though Mandy was the one who had asked for the divorce, it still hurt, for a long time, when she'd see him out and about with someone new. And the women he dated seemed to get younger and younger. The most recent one, Hannah, was only twenty-three years old. Cory was quite proud of that, according to what Mandy heard from some of their mutual friends. They all thought he was an idiot and that Hannah was likely only interested in his money.

Mandy supposed there was some truth to that, but Cory was a good-looking guy too. He was fit and vain, and he still had really good hair. Mandy sighed. She didn't miss Cory as much as she missed what they once had. At one time, they were a close-knit, happy family, and she'd loved chatting with him about his work over dinner. But those days were gone.

Since she'd started dating Matt, she'd discovered that it was nice to have someone ask how her day was for a change. There was always something to talk about with Mimi's Place, and she enjoyed hearing about Matt's boat business too. He was easy to talk to and to laugh with. So far, things were going really well. Sometimes she worried that it almost seemed too easy.

Both Emma and Jill had suggested that she date other people. They liked Matt but were wary of her getting too serious too fast. She understood their concern, but there hadn't been anyone else she'd been interested in dating. She assured her sisters that she and Matt were taking things slow and just really enjoying each other's company. She wasn't looking for anything to change.

It was early still when she walked into Mimi's Place, and no one else was there yet, except for Paul. He was in the kitchen taking inventory before placing a bigger-than-usual order. Their business was way up over prior years, and they expected that this year's Stroll weekend would be even bigger for them than last year. She and Emma and Paul had been planning for months to make sure the weekend was a success.

Paul had really outdone himself with some new menu items, and a special wine dinner was scheduled for the Thursday before the Stroll officially kicked off on Friday. The wine dinner had been Emma's idea and Mandy immediately loved it. Paul was a little hesitant at first but came around when they reminded him he'd have free rein to go bigger and wilder with the menu, if that's where his ideas took him. His first suggestion was to reach out to the Charles Krug winery, which was one of his and Emma's favorites, to see if they'd like to partner and suggest some wines for his menu.

Mandy's contribution was to put some dinner packages together once Paul decided on a prix fixe menu they'd offer for that weekend. It would be one price for a four-course meal, with a choice of appetizer, salad, entrée, and dessert and an optional wine add-on. She made flyers, both paper and digital, and sent them to all the local hotels and bed-and-breakfasts.

As a result, they had a healthy number of reservations booked throughout the weekend. She was confident that they'd also have more walk-ins than usual because the foot traffic along Main Street would be heavy with people strolling along, admiring all the creative holiday window displays, and eventually working up an appetite.

She'd been sad thinking that she wouldn't be able to join the crowds this year. The Nantucket Stroll was always one of her favorite events, and she and the children had a long-standing tradition of putting on their new winter hats and mittens and heading out on Saturday afternoon to explore the downtown area and soak up the Christmas experience. It was magnified when snow was in the forecast and the first few flakes swirled around them.

Their favorite part of the day was when Santa arrived on the coast guard cutter. He walked down the wharf and was then driven to the Jared Coffin House, where the kids would wait in line to sit on his lap. Hers were too big for that now, but they still liked to see Santa arrive, and they loved walking around town, shopping a little and trying the various free samples offered by different stores.

Mandy was glad that Emma had insisted that she still go this year. She was going to have the kids stay with Cory for the entire weekend and skip the festivities, but Emma and Jill assured her they could do without her for a few hours on Saturday afternoon. So, the kids would still be with Cory, but he had agreed to bring them by in the morning and collect them before she needed to head into the restaurant later that afternoon.

Mandy said hello to Paul, then went into her office, settled behind her desk, and opened up her computer and checkbook. Every Monday, she went through and paid the bills. She was just finishing up the last one, for the electric company, when she glanced out the window and felt a thrill at the sight of snowflakes dancing and twirling in the air. It was only the second time they'd seen snow that year. The first had been a brief dusting a few days before Thanksgiving. She checked the weather forecast on her phone and saw that no significant snowfall was expected. The weather was predicted to be cold and mostly clear for the rest of the week with possible flurries again over the weekend. In short, perfect Nantucket Stroll weather.

She collected the stack of stamped envelopes and told Paul she was running to the post office. It was just a short walk away, down by the wharf on Federal Street. The snow was still flurrying a little, and that put Mandy in a festive holiday mood on a Monday, which was usually their quietest day. On the way back to the restaurant, she stopped into the Corner Table café to grab a coffee and got one each for Emma and Paul.

When Mandy returned to the restaurant, Emma was just walking in and smiled at her sister and the coffees.

"Oh, thank you. I was running late and didn't have time to stop and get one." They had very good coffee at the restaurant, but something about getting it from a coffee shop just made it taste better, especially when Mandy splurged on a caramel cappuccino.

"Have you seen the forecast? More flurries for the weekend expected."

Emma looked pleased. "No, I haven't seen that. Good. I'm excited. Paul is too, and he said Jared is working out great. He's glad to have his help, especially for this weekend."

Jared Hawthorne was their newest employee.

He'd started several months ago in the sous-chef role and was Paul's right hand. He came highly recommended after spending five years in a similar role with another Nantucket restaurant that had been recently sold. Mandy hadn't gotten to know Jared well yet. He was very quiet, but he seemed pleasant enough. She had noticed that several of the waitresses seemed to have a crush on him.

He was in his early thirties, and he had the kind of looks that made you pause—dark hair that was slightly too long, deep-green eyes with ridiculously long lashes, a square jaw, and a slight dimple in his chin. If Mandy had been younger, she'd probably have had a crush too.

Jared seemed oblivious to it all, and unlike previous kitchen staff who could be grouchy toward the servers, he was friendly to everyone, which only made the women more interested. They tried to flirt with him, but he didn't seem to take notice and kept his focus on his work.

"Jill and Billy are flying in Wednesday afternoon

and are going to stay through New Year's Eve. They want to help, starting this weekend. Can we add two more to the wine dinner on Thursday? I figured we could put them at our table." Mandy and Emma were going to be overseeing the event and were planning to treat themselves by also partaking in the dinner. Mandy knew once everyone was seated, the servers would be able to easily manage the set menu. She and Emma would be jumping up to help as needed.

"They are? Oh, good. This will be fun. Yes, of course we can include them. I'll let Paul know the final count is plus two."

Mandy and Emma both acted as managers for the restaurant, pitching in as needed and doing just about everything. Emma spent most of her time in the dining room and the kitchen, expediting orders and checking to make sure customers were enjoying their meals. Mandy handled more of the operations work, overseeing the front reservations desk and greeting the regulars.

Their first customer of the day was Connie Boyle, one of their favorite regulars. She had been one of their grandmother's closest friends and lived at Dover Falls, the assisted living community where Grams had also lived. Connie was in her early eighties and was energetic and very social. She came in two or three times a week, often with a few of her girlfriends, but sometimes on her own, especially at lunchtime.

"Hi, Connie, nice to see you. Would you like to sit at the bar today? Or in the dining room by a window?"

Connie thought about it for a moment. "I don't suppose Gina is working?"

"No, she's off today, and she usually works evenings." Gina was an assistant manager and oversaw the bar area. Gina was great and filled in for either Mandy or Emma when they were off. She was very experienced in the restaurant industry and had worked at one of the top Italian restaurants in Boston before moving to Nantucket.

"Okay, then I'll take the window seat, please."

Mandy smiled as she grabbed a menu and led Connie to her table, a small cozy one by a pretty bay window that overlooked Main Street. She knew if Gina had been working, then Connie would have chosen the bar. Gina had that effect on people and had many regulars who knew her schedule and came in specifically to sit at the bar and see her. Gina had a way of making people feel like they were friends, and they loved chatting with her.

"Are you looking forward to the Stroll this weekend? Or will you steer clear of the crowds?" Mandy asked. She knew many of the locals appreciated what the Nantucket Stroll did for the island, but the event was a double-edged sword because the size of the crowds rivaled those of the busy summer season, and many chose to avoid it.

But Connie laughed. "Of course. I'm looking forward to it. A few of the girls and I will be part of the caroling team. We do it every year."

Mandy smiled, picturing Connie and her group

singing festive Christmas carols as they walked along the cobblestone streets downtown.

"That sounds like fun."

"It's great fun! We'll probably stop in for lunch either Saturday or Sunday."

"Wonderful, we look forward to it." Mandy handed Connie the menu and let her know that her server, Stacy, would be right over.

They were busier than usual for a Monday lunch. People steadily stopped in, and the dining room was soon full, with a waiting list. Mandy guessed that there were already people arriving on the island for the holiday weekend and making a vacation of it. She noticed that Connie had set her credit card on her bill and knew Stacy was picking up an order in the kitchen, so she went over to run it for her.

"How was everything?" Mandy asked as she picked up the bill and card.

"Delicious as usual, dear. I almost always get the same thing, you know. Best eggplant parmesan on the island."

Mandy smiled. She knew Connie's love for their eggplant. She'd been surprised when she first started working at the restaurant to discover that most of the regulars ordered the same one or two meals every time they came in.

"Thank you. It's one of my favorites too. I'll be right back with this for you."

She returned a few minutes later with the credit card and receipt and set them on the table along with a pen for Connie's signature. Connie looked thoughtful as she picked up the pen. Mandy was about to walk off to greet a new party that was waiting to be seated when Connie spoke. "It's a shame about Stacy's husband. Terrible time of year to be laid off, and they have three small children too. I hope he finds something soon. She's a nice girl, that Stacy."

Mandy was caught off guard. She hadn't heard about the layoff. She didn't know what to say other than to agree with Connie. "It is a terrible time." She realized that she didn't know what kind of work Stacy's husband did.

Connie looked deep in thought for a moment before smiling and asking, "Your husband does something with finance too, doesn't he? I don't really know what John does, but maybe it's something similar?"

"I'll see what I can find out. Thank you." Mandy felt bad that she hadn't known about the layoff. She imagined it must be a stressful time for Stacy and her family.

Later that afternoon as the shift was winding down and the day servers were getting ready to leave, Mandy walked over to where Stacy was doing her closing side work, rolling silverware into a dinner napkin and stacking the bundles in a bin so they could be easily grabbed for the evening service.

"I was chatting with Connie Boyle, and she mentioned that John was laid off. I'm sorry, Stacy, I had no idea."

Stacy seemed uncomfortable and looked away. "I haven't really talked about it much. I did want to see if there might be any extra shifts I could pick up for the next few weeks. I'm happy to fill in if anyone wants a day off."

"Of course." Mandy thought for a moment, mentally running through the week's schedule. She'd just updated it that morning so it was fresh in her mind. "Would you like to help with the wine dinner? I could use an extra server since the count has gone up. It should be a fun, easy night."

Stacy nodded and looked grateful. "I'd love that, thank you."

"What kind of work does your husband do?"

"He was an analyst with a Boston-based financial services firm. They were just acquired and had a big layoff a few weeks ago. John is one of the newer employees and works remotely, so he was caught in the layoff. He's been sending out résumés, but all the jobs he's finding are in the city."

"I can't promise anything, but if you want to email me a copy of his résumé, I can give it to my ex-husband. His company is headquartered in Boston too, but he works out of the Nantucket office and has a small team here. I don't know if he needs anyone, but I can at least give him John's résumé."

"Really? That would be wonderful. I'll send it to you as soon as I get home."

2

Jill turned at the sound of a bell ringing in the office bullpen, where most of their recruiters sat in an open space. She knew what that meant. She smiled, pushed her chair back, and walked out of her spacious corner office with its floor-to-ceiling glass windows and stunning city views. Her husband and business partner, Billy Carmenetti, was a few steps ahead of her and had his hand up to high-five Emily, their newest hire, on making her first placement.

"Fantastic job, Em. That was a tough one. Did the counteroffer happen the way you expected?"

Emily nodded. She was a pretty woman, in her midtwenties, and this was her first job in recruiting. She'd joined the company after working for several years in marketing at one of the city's top financial services firms. Her salary was good, but she'd been bored with her job and had come in to meet with Billy regarding a search he was working on. Once he met her, Billy had another idea and had Jill meet her too. Without him saying a thing about what he was thinking, Jill made the same suggestion by asking Emily if she'd ever thought about recruiting. She hadn't. But once the idea was presented to her, Emily immediately saw the potential and became excited about the opportunity.

"Yes, it happened exactly the way you and Jill said it would. I told him to expect that he'd get the counteroffer because they wouldn't want to lose him. He didn't believe me because he'd asked for a raise before looking and they'd told him it wasn't possible, that they couldn't afford it. Suddenly they came up with the money. He was flattered enough to sleep on it, but in the morning he realized they'd lied to him and he wondered what else they would lie about, so he knew accepting this offer was the right choice."

"I'm so proud of you, Emily. Hold on…" There was a knock at the front door as Jill went into her office and to the small wine refrigerator that she kept well stocked with various wines—and, for occasions like this, bottles of Veuve Clicquot champagne. She pulled out a bottle and a bag of plastic champagne glasses from her closet, and brought everything back to the bullpen.

Billy was signing a charge slip for the stack of pizzas that had just been delivered. They'd ordered lunch in because Billy and Jill were leaving later that afternoon to fly to Nantucket for the rest of the month. And now they had something to celebrate too. Jill opened the champagne and poured a small amount into each of eighteen glasses so that everyone in the company could toast to Emily's first placement.

Everyone grabbed a slice or two of pizza and gathered in the big conference room. While they ate, Billy led a job-order meeting, where everyone gave status updates on all their open searches and candidate interview activity. When they finished the updates, he grinned and added, "So, any non-work news? How's everyone doing?"

"I came in third last weekend in my first Ironman competition," Rick said shyly. Jill was impressed. Rick was in great shape, but Jill knew how tough the Ironman was: a triathlon where you had to run, swim, and bike. It sounded horrible to her, but she knew placing third was quite an accomplishment.

"Rick, congrats! That is amazing," Jill said.

David, one of their newly married recruiters, reached for his wallet and proudly pulled out an ultrasound picture. "Some of you already know this, but Jenna and I just learned yesterday that we're having a boy!"

The room erupted in a chorus of congratulations and backslapping. Jill caught Billy's gaze, and he grinned and raised his eyebrows. She knew what he was suggesting. He was dying for her to get pregnant. He knew not to mention it again though. She'd made it clear that she wasn't ready yet. Although she'd known Billy for what felt like forever now, that had mostly been as friends and business partners. Being a couple and now married was still new, and Jill wanted to enjoy their alone time for a bit longer, ideally a year or two before they started trying for a baby.

———

Jill and Billy decided to close the office early and give everyone the afternoon off, which was unexpected and much appreciated by the staff. It felt like the right thing to do, since they were ducking out early and wouldn't be there for over a month. They'd still be working remotely part-time from Nantucket so they could keep up with their current activity and hopefully close a few more searches.

Thanks to technology like Zoom, they'd still be able to meet with the team for update meetings.

They'd brought their luggage with them to the office so they could head right to the airport when they left. It was a clear day, cold but sunny. They had a smooth flight to Nantucket and landed a little before four. Mandy was there to pick them up and had the kids with her. Jill loved that Brooke and Blake were so excited to see her. She'd grown close to her niece and nephew during the year that she'd spent on Nantucket, when she and her sisters worked together at the restaurant. She'd been happy to go home to Manhattan when the year was up, but it had been a very good year and a wonderful chance to spend time with her family. They'd all grown closer, and it had been a hard year in some ways for Emma and Mandy. Both were going through divorces, and it helped for all three sisters to be there and support each other.

Jill was glad that Emma was so happy with Paul now, and it sounded like Mandy and Matt were doing well. Both Jill and Emma wondered about that though. Mandy had married Cory soon after college and really hadn't dated much at all. Jill had hoped that once Mandy's divorce was final, she'd get out there and date lots of different men and enjoy herself. Instead, she and Matt found each other, and she didn't seem to have any interest in dating anyone else. Which Jill was pretty sure was a mistake.

Emma was looking forward to seeing her sister Jill and her brother-in-law, Billy. Mandy was picking them up at the airport and had invited her and Paul to join them for dinner. Paul couldn't make it because he had to work, but it was Emma's night off, and she'd made Jill's favorite appetizer, a creamy, hot artichoke-and-spinach dip. When Jill had lived with her at Grams's house for a year, they'd often had the dip as their dinner, along with a glass or two of good chardonnay.

Emma had enjoyed living with Jill. They'd grown closer after years of living on opposite sides of the country. Jill had started the year very much single, while Emma had been trying to mentally process the news that her husband of many years preferred men. She hadn't seen it coming at all, though in retrospect the signs were there. She'd just missed them all because she hadn't ever been looking for them.

But as their grandmother had often said, "Everything happens for a reason," and seeing Paul again was unexpected yet familiar. They'd been childhood sweethearts and had grown apart as young people often do. The years fell away once they began working together, and she suspected her grandmother knew exactly what she was doing when she left Mimi's Place equally to her three granddaughters and her executive chef, Paul. Emma had resisted revisiting the idea of a relationship with him until it was inevitable. Now she couldn't imagine her life without him.

Emma parked in Mandy's circular driveway,

grabbed the dip and bottle of chardonnay from the back seat, and started toward the front door. She paused for a moment to admire Mandy's holiday lighting. The outside of the house and the tall bushes on either side of the front farmer's porch were all decorated with soft white lights. In the distance, just beyond Mandy's house, Emma could see a boat on the water that was also lit up with holiday lights. Through the big bay window that looked into the kitchen, she could see Mandy stirring something on the stove, while Jill and Billy sat at the kitchen island laughing.

She knocked on the door to let them know she'd arrived and walked in. Jill and Billy came over to greet her when she stepped into the kitchen.

"I'm so glad you didn't have to work tonight," Jill said and gave her a big hug. Billy did the same and asked if she wanted a glass of the wine they'd just opened.

"I'd love one, thanks." Emma set her casserole dish with the dip on the stove.

"Is that hot? Or should we pop it into the oven to heat up?" Mandy asked.

"Is that our dip?" Jill said excitedly.

"It is." Emma turned to Mandy. "I think a few minutes in the oven might be good. It's warm, but it could be a little hotter." Mandy popped it in the already-hot oven, next to a bigger pan. "Are those—" Emma didn't even have to finish the sentence before Mandy nodded.

"Yes, the Cape scallops. I haven't had them yet this year, and Jack was just putting them out at Trattel's Seafood when I stopped in."

"Yum," Emma said. Cape scallops were only available for a few months every year. They were smaller than the usual sea scallops and so much sweeter. They were also much more expensive because there was such a limited supply.

Billy handed her a glass of wine as she slid into the open chair at the island, next to Jill. "What's in the pot?" Emma asked as Mandy added some liquid and gave it another stir.

"I'm trying Paul's recipe for lobster and corn risotto. Thought it would go well with the scallops."

"That sounds perfect. Can I do anything to help?" Emma offered.

"No, I'm good. Actually, I think I'm ready for a glass of wine now too. I was drinking tea earlier." She poured herself a glass, gave the risotto a stir, and then checked on the dip, which Emma could see was starting to bubble when Mandy opened the oven door. Emma jumped up to get a platter to put the hot dish on, and Mandy carefully took it out of the oven, set it on the platter, and put it right in front of Jill, who laughed and immediately reached for a toasted pita chip to scoop up the dip.

"This is so good, Em. I haven't had it since we were last here."

"Maybe you should get the recipe and make it for us at home sometime," Billy teased her after he took a bite.

Jill laughed. "I really should do that. So, Emma,

how are things with you and Paul? Any wedding bells on the horizon?"

Emma made a face. She knew Jill was teasing her. "It's going great. I think we'll probably eventually get engaged, but neither one of us is in any rush." She realized that wasn't entirely true. "Well, maybe Paul is ready now. I haven't quite caught up to him. But we're very happy."

Mandy glanced at Jill and Billy. "I'm not sure if I updated you, but we added you both to the list for the wine dinner tomorrow night. You'll be sitting with us. Emma and I are technically working it, but we'll be able to relax and enjoy it too. I added another server, so there's plenty of help."

"Oh, good. We can help too. I hope you're definitely going to put us to work while we're here."

Mandy nodded. "Yes, I've been thinking about that. I thought we could use Billy at the front of the house with me, greeting people and checking reservations, and we can always use you at the bar to give Gina a break."

"Perfect," Jill said. "How is Gina?"

"She's good." Mandy frowned. "I don't think she's all that keen on the holidays. I invited her to join us for Christmas dinner since her family isn't doing anything this year, but she didn't commit."

"They're not?" Jill looked surprised.

"Her mother remarried her father earlier this year. Gina said they are like lovesick newlyweds and are on a cruise around the world. She thinks they'll be somewhere near Spain on Christmas. They invited her to fly in and join them there, but she said that seemed too complicated," Emma said.

"Plus, even though we're closed on Christmas, Gina always likes to work Christmas Eve when all her regulars try to stop in and see her," Mandy added.

"Poor kid," Jill said. "The best part of Christmas is being around family. No wonder she's not feeling it this year. Lots of people dread the holidays, actually."

"I know," Mandy agreed. "I was chatting with

Connie Boyle the other day. You remember, she was Grams's friend?" Jill nodded. "So, she was telling me that it's hard for a lot of the residents at Dover Falls. Some of them either don't have family around or have recently lost their partners, so it's a sad remembrance of what they used to have."

"How is Connie?" Jill asked. "She used to come in often, and I loved chatting with her at the bar. I hope I have that much energy at her age. She seems to really enjoy life."

"She's good. She was telling me how she and a few friends are going to be singing carols during the Stroll."

"Fun! I told Billy he has to get the full Stroll experience. I thought we might make mugs of hot chocolate, slip in a little peppermint or butterscotch schnapps, and walk around counting all the fur coats."

Billy laughed. "Are there really that many?"

"Just wait," Emma said. "You'll see."

"It seems like a million years ago that we used to

do that," Mandy said. She smiled at Billy. "Every time we saw a fur coat, we took a sip."

"And it's a good thing I always made a whole thermos of hot chocolate!" Jill added.

Later, after they finished eating dinner and the kids went up to bed, Mandy opened another bottle of wine, and they settled in the living room by the fireplace. She flipped the switch, and the gas flames roared to life, filling the room with a cheery glow.

Once they were all comfortable, Mandy leaned forward and lowered her voice so the kids couldn't overhear her. "So, I have some interesting gossip. I handed Cory a résumé to take a look at yesterday when he dropped off the kids." She glanced at Emma. "Stacy sent me her husband's résumé. Anyway, once the kids were buckled in the car, Cory pulled me aside and let me know that Hannah, his latest girlfriend, is pregnant."

"Seriously? She's the one who's only twenty-four?" Jill asked.

"Yes. Twenty-three actually."

"Wow. How does he feel about that? What is he going to do?"

"He seemed shell-shocked but a little excited too. I think he's really head over heels for this one. He even mentioned the *e*-word."

"Engaged? Really?" Emma was not impressed. She'd never been crazy about Cory.

Mandy nodded. "It will look better for Cory if he's engaged when she starts to show a baby bump. And having a young wife also looks good."

"And Cory's all about appearances," Emma added.

"Well, I hope he gets a good prenup," Jill said. "Actually, on second thought, I hope he doesn't. Would serve him right."

Mandy laughed. "I don't really know what to think. We'll have to figure out the right time to tell the kids."

"How are you feeling about this? Are you okay?" Jill asked with concern.

"I'm fine. It was a shock at first, but I've moved

on. Cory and I are civil to each other, and he seems happy. As long as he's a good father to the kids, and he is, I have nothing to complain about."

"How is Matt? Are things still good there?" Jill asked.

Mandy smiled. "They are. He's going to join us tomorrow night too. It should be a good time."

3

"Oh good! I was hoping you'd be working tonight," Connie Boyle said as she settled into a seat at the bar. It was exactly 4:35. Connie was right on time. Like clockwork, she came in either Tuesday or Wednesday night, almost every week. Depending on the week, Gina usually worked one of the nights. This week it was Wednesday, but it varied from week to week. She smiled when she saw Connie. She was one of Gina's favorite regulars. The older woman was almost always in an upbeat, cheery mood, and tonight was no exception.

"The usual?" Gina asked as she set a glass of water and a place mat in front of her.

Connie nodded. "Yes, please, with an extra cherry if it's not too much trouble."

Gina smiled as she shook the Southern Comfort Manhattan in a mixer with crushed ice and then strained the drink into an elegant martini glass. She added two maraschino cherries, poured the ice with the leftover cocktail into a rocks glass, and set the glass next to the Manhattan.

"You're the best," Connie said happily as she reached to take a sip.

Another couple came in, and Gina went off to serve them. When she returned to Connie, she was ready to put in her dinner order. She shocked Gina by ordering the swordfish special instead of her usual eggplant parmesan.

"I was here on Monday, so I decided to switch it up a bit," she explained.

"Well, you can't go wrong with Paul's swordfish. It's the best I've ever had," Gina said. Paul had a magic touch when it came to fish. It was easy to overcook, but he always managed to cook it to the perfect point where it was still juicy and melted in your mouth. Gina overcooked fish every time, so she didn't even bother to try anymore. She rang in Connie's order and went into the kitchen to get her garden salad and a basket of hot rolls with butter.

When she returned to the bar, she noticed a new customer had arrived. She didn't look up to see his face until she set Connie's food down. And when she did, she blinked twice in surprise. The man before her was familiar, but she hadn't seen him in years. He looked just as good—maybe better—than she remembered. Alex Scott was a few years older than she was, so maybe thirty-six or thirty-seven now. His hair was thick and blond, and he was as tall and trim as ever. He grinned when he saw her.

"Gina. It's been a long time. You look great."

Connie watched their exchange with interest as she began buttering a roll.

"You do too, Alex. What brings you to Nantucket?"

"I just moved here. I'm starting a new job with the Lawson Group. Maybe you know them?" She did. Mandy's ex-husband, Cory, was one of the owners.

She nodded. "I didn't realize you worked in finance." When she knew Alex, he was a very popular bartender at the same Italian restaurant she'd worked at. He was engaged at the time to Cassie, a beautiful blond waitress, so Gina along with most of the female staff had just crushed on Alex from a distance. Now that she thought about it, he'd been working toward his college degree part-time.

"I finished up a degree in finance a few years ago and got a job as an analyst. Cassie and I broke up. She moved back to California, and this opportunity came along. I thought it might be fun to spend a year or two on Nantucket and... Well, I couldn't pass up the chance to work with Cory Lawson."

"Wow. Congratulations on the new job, and

47

welcome to Nantucket." Gina was aware that Connie was pretending not to pay attention but kept glancing their way. "Can I get you a drink? Would you like to see a dinner menu?"

"I'd love a drink. A Sam Adams IPA if you have it."

"We do." Gina reached into the cooler to get the bottle of beer, opened it, poured half of it into a tall beer glass, and set the glass and bottle in front of him.

He reached into his wallet and pulled out a twenty and handed it to her. "I'm meeting some friends here for dinner. There's five of us, and they have a reservation. I got here a little early. Just walked over from the boat."

Gina noticed a tall black suitcase against the wall.

"I'll keep an eye on that while you eat."

He grinned again. "Thanks. My friend said he'll give me a ride to my rental house. I don't think it's far from here, but with the suitcase…"

"You don't have a car?"

"Haven't had one in years. I lived in the Back Bay and just took Ubers everywhere. Or if we went on a road trip, someone always had a car. Do you think I need one here?"

Gina thought about that for a minute. "Probably not, actually. If you're staying near downtown, you can walk everywhere. And there's Uber here too if you need to get to the airport or want to go elsewhere on the island. Like to Millie's. That's a great Mexican restaurant, but it's on the other side of the island, about a twelve-minute ride by car."

"Mexican, huh? Maybe we can go sometime." He grinned. "You can drive."

She laughed, not sure whether or not he was serious. He took out his phone. "What's your number?" So he was serious. She told him and heard a ping.

"I just texted you so you have my number too. I'll call you in a few days, and we can make a plan. You can be my tour guide. Other than a vacation years ago with some college buddies, I don't know my way around Nantucket at all."

"Okay. Are the friends you're meeting for dinner from Nantucket?"

"One of them is. He's more a friend of a friend. Not someone I know well, but when my buddy Evan heard I was moving here, he insisted I call his friend Chris, so I did. Chris has a few friends in town for something that's going on here this weekend, the Stroll. You've heard of it?"

Gina laughed. "Yes, it's a huge deal here. Should be a very busy weekend."

"Cool." Alex turned at the sound of someone calling his name, and Gina saw a group of guys at the front desk. "Looks like that's my cue to leave. I'll swing by when we're done to say goodbye and grab my suitcase."

Gina felt the buzzer in her pocket go off, the signal from the kitchen that Connie's food was ready. She noticed that Jared, their new sous-chef, was holding two newly filled sodas and was chatting with Connie. Gina hadn't seen him walk up and wondered how long he'd been standing there.

He smiled and nodded her way before heading back into the kitchen. She cleared Connie's salad plate and went to get her swordfish. When she returned a moment later and set the plate down, Connie's drink was almost gone.

"Would you like another Manhattan?" She asked the question to be polite, but already knew the answer.

"Heavens no, dear. If I have another, I'll be plastered! One drink is my limit. Thank you though. Who was that handsome man? Seemed like you knew each other."

Gina smiled. Connie loved to play matchmaker.

"We used to work together in Boston."

"And he's visiting for the Stroll? Or staying longer?"

"He says he just moved here. He got a job at the Lawson Group."

"Oh, isn't that wonderful!" But then a cloud passed over her eyes.

"Is something wrong, Connie? How's your fish?"

"Oh, it's marvelous. It's just… Well, I hope the Lawson Group is still hiring. I think Mandy was going to send Stacy's husband's résumé over there. He just lost his job, you know. Big layoff."

"I didn't know that." Gina immediately felt worried for Stacy. They were about the same age, but as a mother of three small children, Stacy had a very different life from Gina's. Gina knew that money was tight for Stacy's family even with her husband working. Nantucket was not an inexpensive place to live. If he didn't find something soon, Gina guessed they would probably have to move off-island. As glad as she was to see Alex, she hoped that the Lawson Group was doing well enough that they could hire one more person.

Connie ate about half of her meal, and Gina packed up the rest to go.

"I had to save room for tiramisu. Just a small slice, please." They only had one size, and it wasn't small. Connie had no trouble eating all of her dessert though. She was just finishing up when Jared returned to the bar with two empty soda glasses and refilled them. Gina had never seen him at the bar twice in one night.

"You guys worked up a thirst tonight," she commented.

He smiled. "It's hot in there. Busy. That's a good thing though. Should be crazy this weekend. You ready for the Stroll?"

She shrugged. "As ready as I'll ever be, I suppose."

She couldn't really read his expression as he looked at her thoughtfully before finally saying, "What's your favorite part of the Stroll?"

That was easy. "I don't know. I've never gone to it."

Both Jared and Connie looked surprised and disappointed.

"Oh, honey, you have to go this year. At least come Saturday afternoon to hear us sing. I'll be caroling with the girls. It's in the afternoon. You can come then, before you have to go to work," Connie said.

"You really should experience it," Jared agreed.

"Tell you what, why don't you meet me around noon in front of the Straight Wharf restaurant? I'll show you all the highlights, and then you can let us know what your favorite part is."

Gina hesitated. Jared had never said more than a few words to her before. Like the others, she'd noticed how handsome he was, but he was so quiet that she hadn't given him another thought and figured he either had a girlfriend or just kept to himself. But now he and Connie both looked so eager for her to experience the magic of the Nantucket Stroll that she sighed.

"Okay. I suppose I really should check it out so I can talk to customers about it, right?"

Connie looked pleased. "Yes, you should. And I have faith that Jared will take good care of showing you around."

He grinned. "I will. And we'll make sure to find you and listen to your carols."

"Splendid! Well, it's getting late for this old bird. Gina, I'm full up and ready for my check."

"Have a good night, Gina," Jared said before he headed back into the kitchen.

"I like him," Connie said as Gina set her bill down.

"He seems nice. He's new here. I don't really know him very well."

"Well, that will change soon. And that other young man seems pleasant too. I think I prefer Jared though."

Gina laughed. "I think Jared's just being nice. This isn't a date. I'm not sure it's really a date with Alex either."

Connie raised her eyebrows. "Well, whatever you want to call it, I hope you have a good time with both of them. I will expect a full report the next time I come in."

"Okay, Connie. I'll see you on Saturday then, at the Stroll."

Connie beamed. "Yes, you will!"

4

"You're really okay with Cory and his new girl-friend having a baby? How long have they been dating?" Mandy and Jill were sitting in the kitchen Thursday afternoon drinking coffee. The house was quiet because Cory had just stopped by to pick up the kids and Billy was upstairs in the guest bed-room on a Zoom call, interviewing a candidate.

Mandy sighed. "Maybe three months, if that? I'm not going to lie and say I didn't burst into tears the day I found out. As soon as Cory drove off with the kids, I sat there in my car and cried for at least ten minutes. I don't even know why I was crying, exactly, but it felt good. I don't want Cory back, but it's just kind of hard this time of year. It brings out all the emotions, you know? Remembering what we used to have when we were happy and the kids were little. It was a magical time of year. And now it will be for him again, with his new baby and maybe his new wife. It was just a lot to process."

Jill got up and hugged her. "I can't imagine. I'm sorry, Mandy. Sorry that Cory turned into such a jerk. I never really liked him all that much though."

Mandy laughed. "Emma said the same thing. And I do like Matt. I'm glad that we're together."

Jill took a sip of her coffee and was quiet for a moment. "So, it's getting serious then with Matt? I'd hoped you'd have a chance to just have fun and date tons of great men."

"Dating tons of men doesn't sound fun to me. It sounds stressful. It's easy with Matt. I wouldn't say it's serious, but it's very comfortable."

"'Comfortable' doesn't sound very exciting, Mandy. 'Comfortable' is what you say when you're a senior citizen. You're still young." Her sister looked worried.

"I don't mean boring, just that we fit well together. He's easy to be with. It's hard to explain, but I think it's a good thing. I like a quieter life than you do. I don't need a lot of excitement. Manhattan is fun to visit, but I could never live there."

Jill sipped her coffee and smiled. "You're right. Of course, you're right. I just want you to be happy. You deserve that."

"Thanks. And speaking of happy, I'm thrilled for you and Billy. And I'm so glad you two are here through New Year's. We're going to have fun."

"We are. So, tell me about this wine dinner tonight…"

———

The wine dinner was a resounding success.

"Paul really outdid himself," Jill said as they enjoyed the main course, a perfectly cooked filet mignon topped with a rich wild-mushroom demi-glace. They'd started with seared scallops and shrimp over creamy polenta, which was so good.

Mandy, Jill, and Emma had helped the servers bring out each course. Billy had offered to help too, but they insisted they were fine and he should stay and keep Matt company. Gina and Stacy kept every-one's wineglasses full, pouring a different Charles Krug wine for each course. Mandy's favorite was the Generations blend, which was so smooth and went wonderfully with the buttery filet.

The dessert looked amazing as Mandy passed it out. It was some kind of chocolate pastry with lots of cream, pastry layers, and shaved chocolate on top. Mandy was tempted, but didn't take one for herself. She was much too full. Jill and Emma did though—they both loved their sweets. When she went out to dinner, Emma often checked the dessert list before ordering her entrée.

Mandy did, however, have a cup of coffee with a splash of Tia Maria, which was a perfect dessert.

Now that everything had been served, they could relax and take their time finishing up. She noticed that Matt and Billy seemed to be getting along well. Billy could talk to anyone. It came with his job, and Matt was easygoing so she had a feeling they had plenty to talk about.

"How's the dessert?" she asked Matt.

"Very good. Do you want a bite?" He pushed his dish toward her but she shook her head.

"No, I'm good. I'm glad you liked it though."

"I might take Billy out fishing this weekend. He said he's never been ice fishing before. I warned him that it's cold this time of year, and there aren't many fish, but he doesn't seem to mind. It's not bad when we bundle up." He looked excited to go, and Mandy smiled. It didn't sound at all fun to her. She hated being cold. "Well, you guys have fun."

He laughed. "I know I'll probably never get you out there, not this time of year anyway."

"You've got that right."

Billy had the rest of the table laughing at a funny

story about one of his candidates and a recent search that they almost didn't fill when Matt spoke softly so he wouldn't interrupt the others.

"What are your plans for Christmas? Do you have the kids all day or do they go to their dad's too?"

"We were just talking about that the other day. I think the plan is that I'll have them Christmas Eve and then he'll have them for Christmas afternoon and night."

"I'd like to have you over for dinner Christmas night, if that's all right. Your sisters too. Everyone is welcome."

Mandy thought about that for a minute. "Thank you. I definitely want to see you on Christmas too, but why don't you come to my place instead? It might be easier that way since Emma and Paul are going to stop by after he sees his parents and I'm not sure exactly what time that will be."

"Well, if you're sure. I don't want to invite myself."

Mandy gave his hand a squeeze. "I want you there. Thank you for inviting all of us."

Matt relaxed a little. "Okay. Keep my place in mind for New Year's Eve then."

Mandy laughed. "Sure, that's a possibility."

———

Gina's hair was not cooperating. The cold weather seemed to make it take even longer to dry, and she hadn't cut it in a few months so it was longer than usual, almost halfway down her back. It was so thick and wavy that she usually only washed it a few times a week, and it actually looked better on day two or three. But she'd worked the night before and sometimes it seemed her hair smelled like the restaurant—not that Jared was likely to mind that, but she preferred the scent of freshly washed hair and her favorite green-apple shampoo.

She'd just finally finished drying it when the phone rang, and she was surprised to see it was Alex. It was still so strange to think the guy she'd once had such a crush on had moved to Nantucket and walked into her restaurant. And looked just as good as she remembered.

"Morning, beautiful." His voice was cheerful, and she could picture him smiling.

"Hi, Alex."

"Are you still up for showing me that restaurant you mentioned? The Mexican place?"

"Millie's. Yes, of course."

"Great. What night is good for you next week? My schedule is wide-open." He laughed.

"I'm off Tuesday night."

"Okay, Tuesday it is then. Do you mind picking me up? Or I could meet you somewhere downtown. Whatever works for you."

"I'll pick you up." He gave her his address and she jotted it down.

"See you at six then?"

"Six is perfect. See you then, Alex."

Gina was still smiling as she put the phone down and gave her hair a final brush. Just a week ago she'd been feeling down about the holidays and hadn't had a date in weeks, and suddenly she sort of had two lined up with very different guys—though she wasn't sure either was really a date, even though Connie seemed to think so. She hoped that Alex was interested, but she wondered if he was just looking for a friend to show him around. And as cute as Jared was, she wasn't even remotely considering their afternoon at the Stroll to be a date. Not in the slightest. But she was looking forward to it and to seeing what all the fuss was about the Stroll.

She added an extra layer, a warm red cashmere sweater over a snuggly white turtleneck, and her favorite soft jeans and black boots. A red hat, mittens, and scarf, and her long white wool coat, and she was dressed and ready to go. She lived about a half mile from downtown and decided to walk. She knew the area was going to be mobbed, making it nearly impossible to park. Plus, she figured she could use the walk, and it wasn't too bad out. It was cold but sunny, and there was no wind.

She left at a quarter to twelve and made her way

toward downtown and the Straight Wharf restaurant at the beginning of Main Street. She was a few minutes early, but Jared was already there, leaning against the side of a building and watching the crowds. There were already throngs of people of all ages walking around.

Jared smiled and waved when he saw her. He was dressed warmly too in jeans, hiking boots, a hunter-green down jacket, and a navy hat and sweater.

"You made it." His eyes twinkled as he glanced up Main Street toward the group of carolers in front of the old-fashioned Nantucket Pharmacy. "Shall we go hear some carols and say hi to Connie?"

"Sure, lead the way."

Slowly they walked along Main Street, stopping as they went to admire the creative Christmas windows. Each store had decorated its windows and storefront, some with twinkling lights, others with spray snow paint and other decorations. They stepped inside one of Gina's favorite stores, Nantucket Threads, where the owner, Izzy, who was about Gina's age, was handing out samples of hot mulled cider and selling packets of the cider spice mix and all kinds of fun Christmas sweaters and ornaments.

"Cider?" Jared asked as he took one for himself and, when she nodded, handed one to her. Gina took a sip of the hot, sweet beverage that warmed her and tasted like the holidays. She smelled cinnamon and other spices. Gina noticed a few new sweaters—not Christmas ones, just pretty ones that she would have liked to get a closer look at—but didn't want to bore Jared by sweater shopping for herself.

"It looks like you have some new stuff in. I'll stop back in next week," Gina said to Izzy as Jared stepped outside. She followed him, and they continued on their way. Connie saw them as they drew close and waved. A good crowd had gathered around the carolers, and Gina and Jared stayed and listened to several songs before moving on. They were about to step into another store when Jared tapped her arm. "Look, Santa's coming."

A fire truck featuring a waving Santa slowly came down Main Street, which was closed to all other traffic. A line of children ran behind the truck, their parents close behind.

"Where is it going?" Gina asked.

"The Jared Coffin House, I think. That's where the kids will line up to sit on Santa's lap." He glanced at the gift shop straight ahead. "It looks like this store is handing out cookies. Are you interested?"

Gina's stomach rumbled in response, and she laughed. "Yes, please."

They looked around a bit in the store, gratefully accepted a bite-size shortbread cookie, then moved on to Aunt Leah's Fudge Shop, which was handing out samples of their famous fudge and chocolate-covered cranberries, which Gina loved. She bought a small bag of dark-chocolate-covered ones, and they snacked on those as they continued strolling around.

As they walked, she felt the air shift and grow colder, and a few minutes later, fluffy snowflakes started to fall. It was pretty to watch and definitely added to the festive feeling. For the first time in several years, Gina felt a bit of the Christmas spirit.

"Do you like chestnuts?" Jared asked. "I might buy a bag if you'll help me eat them."

"I don't think I've ever had them. I'll try one."

"I'll be right back." Jared bought a paper sack of chestnuts from a street vendor and brought them over to Gina. They sat on a wooden bench and pulled off their mittens, and Jared showed her how to peel the hot chestnuts. They were roasted with an X scored into their bottoms, which made it easy to pull off the outer shell. The nut inside was soft and starchy and unlike anything Gina had tried before. It was an unusual taste, but she liked it and reached for another. They polished off the rest of the bag and got up to keep exploring.

Ten minutes later, they turned a corner and Jared glanced her way.

"Any interest in cookie decorating?"

Gina looked toward the sign that Jared was

looking at. Cookie decorating was about to start in a few minutes.

"Sure, let's do it."

Long tables were lined up along the sidewalk for the cookie decorating. Big Santa sugar cookies waited on paper plates, and every few feet there were squeeze bottles of frosting and shakers of sugar glitter. They had a blast decorating their cookies, and after Gina took a selfie of them holding up their creations, Jared immediately bit into his and she did the same. They continued nibbling as they walked along, taking in all the sights.

A group of three women strolled past them, all wearing glossy mink coats. Two other women came toward them in very warm-looking brown beaver coats. The groups of women all waved to one another.

Gina laughed once the women were out of sight. "I've never seen so many fur coats in my life."

"Well, it is Nantucket. Can't have the Stroll without everyone showing off their fur coats," he agreed. "I could actually go for a hot coffee. Want to stop into the Corner Table and warm up for a bit?"

"That sounds good." The Corner Table café was right around the corner on Federal Street, and it was busy, but after they got their coffees, a table by the window opened up, and Gina scooted over to get it while Jared followed with their coffees. They settled down and took off their coats.

Gina was curious to learn more about Jared. She knew he'd lived on the island longer than she had.

"What drew you to Nantucket?" she asked.

"We used to have a summer place here when I was growing up. My parents divorced ten or so years ago, and my mother decided to move here. I was working on the Cape, at a restaurant in Chatham, and about five years ago, I was just ready for a change. My mother said she loved being here year-round. I always loved it here and missed seeing her."

Gina nodded. "That's one downside of living here. It's not convenient to go off-island."

"Right. It's easier if you live here than to try and visit someone who lives here. My mother used to live in Duxbury, and I could just zip up from the Cape to see her. I hardly ever go off-island now, and I'm pretty happy here. It's more laid-back, yet there are still some really high-end restaurants."

"You're liking it so far at Mimi's Place?"

"It's great. I'm learning a lot from Paul. Eventually, I want to have my own restaurant, but I know I'm not ready yet. Maybe in a few more years."

That intrigued her. Jared sounded passionate about what he did. She admired that. "What will your place be like? Have you thought about it?"

"All the time. I think it will be small, more of a bistro, with all fresh herbs. I have an herb garden and love using fresh herbs. The flavor is just so good. I see it as elegantly casual, so not stuffy but the kind of place you can relax and enjoy really good food."

"That sounds great. Do you have any other family here, any brothers or sisters?"

He shook his head. "No, it's just me."

"And you live with your mom?"

"Sort of, but not really. There's a guest house, a small cottage on the property, and that's where I'm staying. My mother wanted me to live in the main house with her, but this way we each have our own space, and I'm nearby in case she needs me."

"That sounds perfect. I'm in a cottage like that too. It was a caretaker's cottage on a big estate. It's perfect for one person and the rent was relatively affordable—for Nantucket."

"Are you dating anyone?" Jared asked casually and reached for his coffee.

Gina hesitated, then chose her words carefully. "I haven't been recently. I have a first date next week though."

He nodded. "That guy you were talking to at the bar the other night?"

"Yeah. He's someone I knew in Boston. We worked together years ago, but we never dated before. He was with someone else then. What about you?"

"I'm not dating anyone. I was pretty serious with someone for several years, but we broke up a few months ago. She moved off-island, said she couldn't see herself living here long-term."

"It's not for everyone," Gina agreed. "I love it here, but I've had a few times where I've wondered too, like when the boats aren't running. I had to go to a funeral a few months ago and almost didn't make it off-island. I got on the last plane before they stopped flying and then had to rent a car in Hyannis. It was stressful."

"Do you see yourself staying here now? Or do you still think you might want to move back to Boston?"

"I love it here. I think it would be hard to live in Boston again after being here. It's a special place."

Jared smiled. "It is. Are you working tonight? I just noticed the time, and we should probably get going. It's after three." They both had to be in by four.

"Oh, I didn't realize it was so late." Gina stood

and grabbed their empty coffee cups and dropped them in the trash.

"How did you get here? I think you said you were going to walk. I drove, so I can give you a ride home if you like. That will save you some time."

"I did walk, and I'd love that, thanks."

She followed Jared to his Jeep, which was parked by the supermarket. She climbed in, and a few minutes later, he pulled into her driveway.

"I had a really fun time. Thank you for making sure I experienced the Nantucket Stroll."

"I'm glad you came. It was fun for me too. See you at work."

5

Jill glanced out the big bay window in Mimi's Place and marveled at the size of the crowds streaming by. Christmas Stroll felt even busier than summertime because it was so concentrated over one weekend. She and Billy had checked it out the day before, Friday afternoon, before heading in for their first shift. The fun holiday activities had put both of them in a festive mood. And she'd been impressed by how well Billy picked things up at the reservations desk. He'd worked at a restaurant briefly during college, and even though that was years ago, it came right back to him. She could hear him now as he greeted Connie Boyle and two of her girl-friends, who, by the looks of their outfits, had just finished caroling for the day.

"Don't you ladies look beautiful and so festive. We have a table by the window that I think you'll enjoy. You can watch the Christmas crowds strolling by."

"That sounds perfect! You must be Billy, Jill's husband."

Jill smiled at the surprise in Billy's voice when he answered, "Why yes, I am."

"I thought so. I'm Connie Boyle, one of the regulars here, and I was a friend of the girls' grandmother. Mandy said you'd be working this weekend."

"We're actually here through New Year's Eve, so you might see even more of me." He turned on the charm as only Billy could, and the three ladies beamed at him as he led them to their table. He handed them menus, and they looked up as Stacy came over.

"You're in good hands now. Enjoy your lunch, ladies."

It was really more of an early dinner or late lunch as it was a quarter to four, which was kind of an in-between time when service was slow and they normally changed shifts and got ready for the evening service. But today was different. Billy, Jill, and Emma were all working double shifts, while Mandy was taking the kids to the Stroll. The lunch service had been mobbed earlier, as expected.

Even now, there were a few scattered tables throughout the dining room, but it was much quieter. Jill smiled to herself, thinking that it was like the calm before the storm. The bar was almost empty; there was just one older couple having Irish coffees. Jill had worked the bar by herself for lunch, as Gina was off experiencing the Stroll for the first time. She was due in any minute, and the bar would be much busier in the evening.

The window table where Connie and her friends were sitting was in earshot of the bar, and while Jill cut fruit to prep for the evening shift, she couldn't help overhearing their conversation with Stacy.

"Hello, dear. Have you had a chance to take your kids to the Stroll yet?" Connie asked.

"Yes, we went earlier today so they could all sit on Santa's lap. And, Connie, I really owe you a thank-you. John was hired by the Lawson Group yesterday."

"Oh, that's marvelous news! You don't need to thank me for that though."

Stacy smiled. "Yes, I do. I know you said something to Mandy, because I hadn't. And she sent John's résumé to Cory Lawson. It's much appreciated."

Connie beamed. "Well, I'm so glad it worked out, dear."

Stacy was taking their order when a customer came to the bar and Jill went over to greet him.

Ten minutes later, Mandy walked in and stopped by the bar to say hello to Jill.

"Are you ready for the mad rush? They should start pouring in soon."

Jill smiled. "I'm ready. Did you have fun with the kids today?"

"Yes, they loved it. Especially the cookie decorating and eating. Thanks again for covering for me."

"Of course. So, I just overheard that Cory hired Stacy's husband. That's great news, and a little surprising. Is he turning into a softy suddenly?"

Mandy laughed. "Hardly. I was worried that he wouldn't be able to add another person, but he seemed excited when he saw John's résumé and told me this morning that he hired him almost without talking to him. He has a unique skill set, and Cory knows people at the company John worked at. He did a backdoor reference, and they raved about him. Cory said he expects that John will help make the company a lot of money."

Jill nodded. "Now that sounds more like Cory. I'm glad it worked out. Stacy is really sweet."

"She is. Oh, I'd better run. They're starting to come in."

Jill glanced toward the front desk, where Billy was grabbing a stack of menus to seat a family, and there was another party of three waiting behind them. As Mandy left to help, she passed Gina on her way in. Gina's cheeks were pink from the cold, and her long black hair was up in a ponytail, tied with a red velvet ribbon. Like Jill, she was wearing a crisp white button-down shirt, black pants, and a black apron.

"Love the hair tie. You look very festive. What did you think of the Stroll?"

Gina smiled. "It was great. I get it now. I'm glad I went."

They didn't have much time to chat after that because the bar filled up with people waiting for their reservations or walk-ins hoping they could eat at the bar.

Jill recognized a lot of people from the year she spent working at the restaurant. Most of them remembered her too and said they were glad to see her home for the holidays. She was impressed by what a good job her sisters and Paul had done since she'd gone back to Manhattan. Mimi's Place had so many loyal regulars now, and business was booming.

"Jill, Mandy mentioned you were back in town! Nice to see you." Kate Hodges and her sister Abby were at the bar waiting to order drinks. Their sister Kristen waved from the other side of the room where she was standing with her boyfriend, Tyler, Kate's husband, Jack, and Abby's husband, Jeff.

"Hey, great to see you all too! Billy and I are here through the holidays. It's nice to be home. What can I get for you?"

Kate placed their order, and Jill quickly poured their drinks and set them on the counter. Kate gathered a few of them up while Abby stayed to pay the bill and carry the rest.

"How's Natalie?" Jill asked as she set down Abby's change. She rarely saw Abby without her young daughter.

"She's great. She's with my mom tonight so I could have an adult night out. My mom would love to see you all. She's having her big holiday open house next Sunday. You should all stop by. It will go all afternoon."

"Thanks. I'd love to, and I'll mention it to the others."

"Great. See you soon." Abby wandered off, carefully holding her three drinks, and Jill turned her attention to the next person in line. The bar was three deep with people wanting drinks. She took a deep breath and smiled. "What can I get for you?"

Usually the restaurant emptied out by ten thirty on weekends, but it was a little past eleven by the time the last customer left. The staff that didn't have to rush home gathered at the bar for an after-work drink. Usually if there was more than one bartender working, they split all the tips equally, but before the others arrived at the bar, Jill told Gina the money was all hers. Gina protested. "That doesn't seem right. You did as much as I did."

Jill smiled. "And I'm an owner, so it's all good. You worked hard and deserve it."

Gina still looked unsure but nodded. "Okay. Well, thank you. People were very generous tonight."

"What are you drinking?" Jill asked as she poured herself a glass of Josh cabernet.

"I'll have a chardonnay, the Bread and Butter. Thanks." Once their wines were poured, they brought their glasses to the other side of the bar and sat. As Mandy, Billy, and the others made their way over, Jill and Gina took turns jumping up to make their drinks. Jill noticed with interest that the new guy in the kitchen, Jared, took the seat next to Gina.

Mandy lifted her glass in a toast. "To our best night ever. We set a new record."

"That's awesome!" Jill knew it had been busy, but she hadn't realized the night had been that good.

"More than half of the guests ordered Paul's prix fixe menu," Emma said proudly.

Paul looked pleased too. "That was a nice surprise. We might want to think of offering that more often, maybe on a regular basis. The profit margins are higher, and it made things go more smoothly in the kitchen."

"And people like it because they get a better deal than buying everything separately," Mandy said. "I got a lot of positive feedback from the hotels and bed-and-breakfasts when I sent the flyers out, but I really didn't know it would do so well."

"Except for the screaming baby at table two, things went great in the dining room too," Emma said.

Jill laughed. "I could hear that baby from here. The poor mother."

Mandy looked sympathetic. "I've been in her shoes. It's not always easy taking small children to restaurants. We didn't do it very often when the kids were that little. It's too stressful wondering if they are going to have a meltdown and then embarrass us when they do."

"You were always good though," Emma said. "You'd take them right outside until they calmed down. Some parents don't do that."

"I don't know how they can just ignore it," Jill said. "It seems like they just scream louder until the parent finally pays attention to them. And you wonder why I'm not in a hurry to have kids," she joked. But when she glanced Billy's way, he wasn't laughing.

"It's different when they're your own," Mandy assured her. "You find your own rhythm. Some kids are better about going out than others. Finding a good babysitter is a blessing."

"Oh, that reminds me. Did you see the Hodges sisters? Kate and Abby stopped at the bar to get some drinks and invited us all to their mom's open house. It's next Sunday at the Beach Plum Cove Inn, and we're all invited."

Mandy smiled. "I didn't make it last year, but when she's had her open houses in prior years, I've often stopped in. Lisa Hodges knows how to throw a party. The food is always really good."

6

"Are you sure you don't mind that I'm going out with Matt tonight? He said you two are welcome to join us. I wish you would." Mandy felt like a terrible hostess abandoning her houseguest sister to go out for a romantic dinner.

But Jill laughed. "Don't be silly. I insist. We'll have plenty of time to see Matt too, and we don't have to do everything together. You need a date night with just the two of you."

"Okay. Well, there's plenty of food in the fridge, or you can always get takeout."

"Billy will probably want pizza. We have pizza

at least twice a week. But I like it too, so it works for us."

Matt arrived a little before seven, and they headed off to one of their favorite Monday night restaurants, Crosswinds at the airport. It was a favorite spot for locals, had a cozy pub feel, and featured good comfort food. Matt ordered his usual local beer, Cisco's Shark Tracker, and Mandy had a glass of Bread & Butter cabernet, which was her new favorite. Matt got the meat loaf, and Mandy went for the roast chicken with mashed potatoes and gravy. She rarely ordered chicken at restaurants, but she liked how they did it here, and the weather was so cold and raw outside that roast chicken sounded good.

The restaurant was busy but not too crowded. Monday night typically was one of the slowest, and many restaurants took it as a day off and closed completely. But Crosswinds never closed. Mandy guessed it was partly because they were at the airport and people would need somewhere to go while waiting for flights. She was glad they were open. It was a cheery and welcoming place, and they were decorated for Christmas with a tree in the corner, and garlands and lights pinned around the room.

Nancy, the older waitress who often served them, always remembered their order. She brought a basket of rolls out and, not too long after, delivered their meals, which were delicious, as usual.

As they ate, Matt told Mandy that as long as the weather stayed cold, he was planning on taking Billy ice fishing on Sunday.

"There's a group of us going. It should be a good time."

"Ice fishing. So you'll literally stand over a hole in the ice hoping to catch a fish?" It did not sound at all fun to Mandy.

But Matt seemed excited about it. "Yes, pretty much. We'll have a cooler of beer and food, so it will be a good time."

She smiled. "I'm sure Billy will love it."

"He'll fit right in."

"Hi, Matt! I thought that was you."

Mandy and Matt looked up to see a very attractive woman walking their way. She smiled when she caught Matt's eye. Mandy thought she looked vaguely familiar, maybe just from seeing her around town. Her hair was glossy and a rich, deep brown. It was cut in flattering layers and fell just past her shoulders. Her makeup was minimal, but she didn't need much; her skin glowed, and she had high cheekbones and big brown eyes. She looked effortlessly chic in her crisp white shirt and tailored gray pants. And she carried a gorgeous camel-colored Birkin bag. She looked like Nantucket old money, and for a moment Mandy felt a bit frumpy in comparison.

"Amy, nice to see you. Do you know my girlfriend, Mandy Lawson? Mandy, Amy works next door to my office."

Amy glanced her way and nodded. "Nice to meet you. I'm the building office manager." She turned to Matt. "Did you like the present I left for you?"

Matt laughed. "Yes, I ate every crumb. That was unnecessary but kind of you. Thanks again."

"Well, I'm off to meet my friends. You two have fun."

Amy walked off, and Mandy raised her eyebrows. "She made you a present?"

"She likes to bake. She made lemon cakes for all the guys at the boat basin."

"Isn't that nice." Mandy wondered how old Amy was. "Is she single?"

"I don't really know. Maybe? She goes out with her friends a lot. Seems like everywhere I go, Amy is there."

"Interesting." Matt was a catch, and at forty-four, he was plenty young enough to start a new family with someone. He didn't show any interest in Amy though, and Mandy really didn't think she had to worry about that with him. But then she thought of Cory and his very pregnant young girlfriend and lost her appetite. She picked at her dinner, while Matt inhaled the rest of his. He noticed that she wasn't eating much.

"Is your chicken okay?"

"It's fine. Delicious as usual. I'm just not that hungry, I guess." She took another bite and set her fork down. "Did I tell you Cory might be getting engaged soon? His young girlfriend is expecting."

"Oh! Wow." Matt took a sip of his beer and looked at her closely. "Is that what's bothering you?"

She shook her head. "Not anymore. I wasn't sure how I felt about it when I first heard. It's strange to think that Cory is basically going to start over. He might have several kids, who knows? You could do that too. I bet Amy would be up for it."

He reached over and took her hand and squeezed it. "I'm not interested in Amy. And I think kids are great, but mine are in college. The thought of starting over again makes me tired." He looked into her eyes. "Unless you really wanted more. Then I could find a way to get on board. You're still young enough if that's what you wanted to do."

Mandy laughed. "Oh my goodness, that's the last thing I want. I love my children, but I agree with you. The thought of doing it all again—diapers, sleepless nights… No, thank you."

Matt looked relieved. "Good. I'm glad we are on the same page."

Mandy was very glad too and relieved that Matt said he had no interest in Amy. Because it was clear to Mandy that Amy was interested in Matt. She thought it was brazen of her to walk up while they were having dinner together and to mention in front of Mandy that she'd given Matt a gift. Who did that? And Mandy had been wondering what to do about a gift for Matt. She wanted to get him something meaningful but not too much or too little. She needed to check with Jill and Emma for ideas. She had no idea what would be appropriate after dating someone for three months, but she wanted to get him something special.

7

Gina stared at her closet for a good ten minutes, trying to decide what to wear for her night out with Alex. She still wasn't sure if it was meant to be an actual date, so it felt silly to be so worried about what to wear, but she couldn't help it. It had taken her all of two seconds to decide what to wear when she met Jared at the Stroll, but she knew that wasn't a date, so it was different. There was no pressure, no expectations. She'd been surprised by what a fun day it had turned out to be. Jared was a nice guy and the time had flown by.

Boots, her all-black cat with four white paws,

sat on Gina's bed watching her intently in between yawns. She was in her usual afternoon nap spot, on Gina's pillow.

Gina tried on a few different tops, then settled on a navy-blue V-neck sweater and jeans. Her outfit was casual, but the sweater was a nice one and flattering. It was a good color for her, and she always felt confident when she wore it. She added a swipe of rosy-pink lipstick, grabbed her coat and purse, and headed out. She punched Alex's address into her phone's GPS, connected it in the Jetta's console, and, a few minutes later, pulled up to his house on Orange Street.

His rental was an apartment that was part of a very old house. It was a convenient location within easy walking distance to downtown and the Lawson Group's office. Alex was outside, talking on his phone, and looked up when he heard her car. He ended the call, walked over, and got into the passenger side.

"Thanks for coming to get me." He looked and

smelled great. She couldn't place his cologne, but it smelled freshly applied, and she guessed from the dampness of his hair where it met the collar of his shirt that he'd recently showered too.

"You're welcome. How's the new job going?"

"Great so far." He told her all about his new role and how awesome the company was while they drove to Millie's. "In a couple of years, if all goes well, I'll move into the top spot as a portfolio manager. That's where the real money is, although it can be good at my level too, as a senior analyst. The guys are great. Two of us started yesterday."

"Oh, is the other one John? One of the girls at the restaurant said her husband just got hired there."

"That's him. Seems like a smart guy. Kind of on the quiet side."

Gina pulled into the lot, and they went into Millie's and upstairs where the view of the ocean was better, though it was dark by now. They sat at a high-top table in the bar, and both ordered margaritas and some guacamole and chips to snack on while they decided what else to have. Alex went with a beef burrito and Gina decided on scallop-and-bacon tacos.

"So, you're still working in the restaurant business," Alex said when the waiter set down their drinks and appetizer. "Did you go to college for hospitality?"

Gina smiled. "No. I kind of fell into it. I was a fine arts major. At one point I thought about teaching art, but I ended up liking the fast pace of restaurant work. I really like the mix of what I do now, mostly managing the bar and covering for the dining room and front-desk managers on their nights off."

Alex nodded. "I never minded it, but I was ready to get a real job once I graduated. Not that restaurant work isn't a real job. It just wasn't what I wanted for a career."

"I knew what you meant. I'm glad you found something you love to do. You used to play hockey too, I think, didn't you?"

He grinned. "Yeah, I was on a men's league. My brother was too. We both played in high school."

"There's an active men's hockey league here. You might want to look into it."

"No kidding? That's awesome. Thanks for letting me know. What else should I know about Nantucket? Tell me all your secrets."

Gina laughed and then told him a few of her favorite places and the best days to go there.

"Oh, if you do get a car, don't bring it with you when you go off-island. You'll have to take the Steamship Authority's slow boat, which takes twice as long as their high-speed ferry. It's easier and faster to take the fast ferry from here and then either call for an Uber or rent a car if you're going over the bridge." When people left the Cape to go to Boston or elsewhere, they had to cross the Cape Cod Canal, so it was often referred to as "going over the bridge," which was a big deal and a rare thing for many native Cape Codders.

"I went to college with a girl from the Cape," Gina said. "After graduation, she got a job in Hyannis. I tried to get her to visit me in Boston and finally, once, she did. But she got so lost. She ended up taking a wrong turn and ended up in Chelsea, and I had to stay on the phone with her while she drove to my place. I think that was the last time she crossed the bridge."

Alex laughed. "My mom's friend is like that too. I can't imagine." The waiter arrived with their food and they dug in. As they ate, Alex caught her up on some of the people they both knew from the restaurant in Boston. He still saw some of them even after he graduated and started working in finance.

When they finished eating, Alex ordered another margarita but Gina still had more than half of hers left. She sipped it slowly to make it last. She didn't want another one. They were big and she was always careful when she was driving. Plus, she was so full.

Alex took a sip, then yawned and immediately apologized. "That was rude. I'm sorry. I'm still getting used to the hours. I had a few weeks off before starting this job, and I fell into sleeping late and not getting up until seven."

"Seven? That seems early to me. What time do you have to be in the office?"

"We're there by seven at the latest, so I'm usually up by around five or so to check the markets and work out before heading in. It's a long day. Everyone was still there when I left at six thirty. I'll probably stay 'til seven or so tomorrow."

"That's a twelve-hour shift." It sounded like a very long day.

"Yeah, the norm is a sixty- or seventy-hour week. It's intense, but I love it."

She could tell that he really did, and his energy was contagious. She thought about her artwork. She hadn't painted anything in months. She was always so tired when she got home from work. But she did love painting and she missed it. She made a mental note to make time for it and to start a new painting soon.

"Do you want dessert?" Alex asked when the server came back to their table.

Gina shook her head. "No, thanks. I'm stuffed.

But if you want something go ahead. They have a really good key lime pie."

Alex yawned again. "I think I'll pass too. Maybe next time?"

Gina thought it was a good sign that he mentioned a next time, a second date possibly. When the bill came, Gina pulled out her wallet, but Alex insisted on paying.

They left, and when she dropped him off, he leaned over and kissed her cheek. "Thank you for driving. I had fun tonight and you were right: Millie's is great."

"I had a good time too. Thanks again for dinner."

"It was my pleasure." He paused for a moment. "Do you ever have a weekend night off?"

"Sometimes. I usually take every other Friday night, but I can also switch a night or ask for a night off if I know ahead of time."

"There's a company Christmas party the Friday after this one. Would you like to go with me? It's supposed to be a big deal. They have it at the

Whitley Hotel. I'm not familiar with it, but they say it's impressive. And everyone is bringing a date. It should be fun, I hope."

Gina had never been to the Whitley, but she'd heard about it. It was a waterfront, ultra-exclusive hotel on the other side of the island. She was curious to see what all the fuss was about and excited for another date.

"I'd love to go with you."

"Great, I'll give you a call soon. Maybe we can see a movie or something before then."

"Good night, Alex."

8

"You look comfy." Paul's voice was amused as he stood in the living room doorway, holding a mug of coffee and looking at Emma, who was curled up on the sofa with a soft knit throw over her lap, her fluffy Maine coon cat in her lap and Paul's giant orange boy, Brody, snuggled up next to her. She'd adopted her cat from a local shelter. She was an older kitty, almost seven and her full name was Isabella. They'd called her Izzy at the shelter and Emma and Jill had at first too, but that soon morphed to Bella, which seemed to suit her better. There were also her nicknames: Bella-boo, Bellery,

Baby Belle. Paul laughed at the many different names Emma's cat answered to.

Emma smiled. "We are very comfy." She took a sip of her spicy cinnamon tea and glanced outside where a blanket of white covered the ground and trees and tiny icicles hung from the window frame. She could almost feel the cold, and she wasn't looking forward to venturing out. But they were both due at the restaurant by four, and a quick glance at her phone told her time was running out.

"I suppose I should jump in the shower. You might have to take over my spot."

He laughed. "I can do that." Paul's hair was still damp from his own shower, and he was already wearing the long-sleeved T-shirt and heavy sweatpants that he wore in the kitchen under his white chef's jacket. Emma carefully got up, so as not to disturb the "children," as she and Paul referred to the two cats. Paul settled into her spot and Emma quickly showered, changed, and blew her hair dry.

They often walked to work. Her grandmother's house, where they lived, wasn't far from downtown. But it was so bitter cold out that they decided to drive instead. Emma warmed the car up, and a few minutes later, they arrived at Mimi's Place.

Gina was already behind the bar, putting away a case of wine, and Jason and Jared were in the kitchen. Jason, the lunch chef, was taking off his white coat and getting ready to leave for the day, while Jared was putting his on.

Paul headed into the walk-in refrigerator to take a look at what they had on hand for the evening and decide what to do for a special. Sometimes specials were a limited supply of seafood that just came in or a creative way to move an item they had extra of.

Emma hung up her coat and joined Mandy, Billy, and Jill at the front desk. They were about to leave for the day too. Mandy handed her the reservations book. "It was busy today and we took more reservations than usual for tonight. Some people asked about the prix fixe menus when they called. I already let Jared know so he and Paul can make sure they have some good options for tonight."

"Great, thanks. What are you two up to tonight?"

"Cory is bringing the kids by soon, and we are going to hunker down and watch some Christmas movies, I think. Maybe get pizza or Chinese take-out. None of us feels like cooking."

"I don't blame you. It's a good night for that. Have fun."

Emma was initially surprised that they were busy earlier than usual. Connie Boyle wasn't the only one who came in around four thirty. By a little past five, the dining room was more than half-full and most of the people had at least one shopping bag with them. And the early people were almost all walk-ins. She guessed they worked up an appetite walking around and shopping.

When there was a lull in new customers, Emma strolled over to the bar to say hello to Gina. Jared was by the soda gun, filling up a tall glass with ice and coke. Connie looked up when she saw Emma.

"Hello, dear. I was just asking Gina how her date with that nice young man went. But she seems suddenly shy to tell us."

Jared chuckled as Gina looked like she wanted to crawl under the bar. "Yes, Gina, how was your date?" he asked. "We're all dying to know."

Emma sensed something in the air but wasn't quite sure what it was. She felt a little bad for Gina. "It's really none of our business. Gina doesn't have to tell us anything." She grinned. "Though we are curious."

Gina relaxed and laughed. "It's not that big a deal. We had a nice time. We went to Millie's. I'd suggested it as one of my favorite places."

"And what did he think?" Jared asked.

"He liked it."

Jared nodded. "Millie's is one of my favorites too. Glad you had a good time. I'll catch up with you all later."

As soon as Jared was back in the kitchen, Gina sighed. "Well, that was awkward."

"Why? I'm glad you had a good time," Emma said.

"She means because of Jared," Connie said with an impish look.

"Oh?"

"Jared and I are just friends," Gina said. But Emma noticed a red flush creeping over her cheeks. How interesting.

"I like Jared," Emma said. She knew Paul thought highly of Jared, and he'd been friendly and polite to Emma, though a little quiet, so she really didn't feel like she knew him well.

"That's what I told her too," Connie said. "It's good for them to know about each other. Keeps them on their toes."

"Oh, how sad," Gina said. The television above the bar was on and was showing a small Nantucket family, a mother and two young children, who had to be evacuated to a local hotel when the pipes unexpectedly burst in their rental house and flooded the entire downstairs. Her husband was in the army and not expected home for months, and there was extensive water damage.

"Saddest of all, this young mother had done her Christmas shopping early and had everything wrapped and ready for the holiday, safely stored in the basement, and now it's all floating in several inches of water. She can't afford to replace everything. Please be aware of the dangers of frozen pipes this time of year."

"How awful." Emma's heart went out to the poor mother, who looked completely frazzled and disheartened. "I wonder if there's a fund set up to help."

Just as she was asking, a number flashed across the screen and the announcer said, "You can also check our website for details on how to donate."

"Something like that happened to me years ago, when I was newly widowed. It was a very difficult time, but people are good, and an angel helped. I'm sure the same will happen for that young lady," Connie said.

"I hope so," Emma said and made a mental note

to look up the information on the website when she got home, and send in a donation.

Later that night, as they were getting ready to close, Emma walked to the bar to get Gina's sales total for the night. Gina was wiping down the counter, and Jared was leaning on it, and Emma overheard him as she approached.

"Since you hadn't gone to the Stroll before, I suppose you didn't check out the Festival of Trees at the Whaling Museum last year either? It goes all month."

Gina laughed. "You guessed right. I've heard it's wonderful though."

"We could check it out this Saturday afternoon before work if you want."

Gina hesitated. "I can't do Saturday. But I could do Sunday."

Jared looked pleased. "Sunday it is. Have a good night, Gina."

And now Emma knew what it was she'd sensed earlier. Something was brewing between these two.

9

"Meow!"

Gina looked up from her painting to see Boots inching closer, wearing an indignant expression. The small cat meowed again, louder and more insistent this time.

"Okay, hold on a minute." Gina set her paintbrush down and followed Boots and her rapidly twitching tail into the kitchen. The cat stopped short by her food bowl and glared up at Gina. The bowl was totally empty. Gina had been so engrossed in her painting that she'd forgotten to put breakfast out for Boots.

"I'm sorry, honey." She opened a can of wet food and dumped it in the cat's bowl, and Boots began attacking it as if she'd been starved for days. Gina added a small dish with some dry food too, so Boots could snack if she got hungry later. She usually always had some food in that bowl, but it had been bone dry too.

Feeling like a horrible cat mother, Gina scratched behind Boots's ears and then made her way back to the easel where her half-finished painting sat. She'd started right after she had her coffee and had been so into her work that she'd lost all track of time. It felt good to paint again. She needed to pick up some new paints and brushes though, because hers were not in the best shape. They'd been neglected for too long.

She painted for a little while longer, then jumped in the shower to get ready to meet Alex at the movie theater. The Dreamland was the only option for movies on Nantucket and usually had one big movie and two more artsy ones showing at any given time. Gina had checked the listings and was hoping that Alex might be interested in one of the smaller movies because they both sounded great to her. The main film was an action thriller starring Tom Cruise.

Gina dressed casually in jeans and a big warm sweater and turtleneck because it was bitterly cold out. She pulled on her mittens, hat, and coat and made her way over to the Dreamland, which was just off Main Street. One thing she loved about Nantucket was that just about everything was an easy walk downtown. She still liked having her car though, for going to the bigger supermarket, Stop & Shop, or over to Millie's or Barrett's Farm.

Alex was waiting outside by the front door. He held up two tickets.

"I went ahead and got the tickets for us."

"Oh, great. Which movie did you get?"

"The Tom Cruise one. I figured that's the one you'd want to see. Is that okay?"

She smiled. "Of course. I'll get the popcorn."

She was a little irritated that Alex didn't wait to ask which movie she wanted to see, but she got over it quickly as she waited in line for the popcorn. She got a bag for each of them and two waters.

The movie was actually pretty good. Alex laughed every time she jumped in her seat. She couldn't help it; she always got so into the movie that she was on edge and jumpy with any suspense thriller. It was fun though and the popcorn, as usual, was excellent. When the movie finished, they walked down to the Corner Table to share a coffee. Alex got a giant sugar cookie too, and Gina agreed to help him eat it.

"Are you going home for the holidays?" he asked as he broke off a piece of cookie and popped it in his mouth.

"No. My parents are actually on a cruise. They invited me to fly to Spain to join them, but that's too complicated. And I usually work Christmas Eve. A lot of the regulars come in, and it's a fun time. What are you doing?"

"Our office shuts down early on Christmas

Eve, and I'll take the ferry to Hyannis and then rent a car to go to my parents' place in Concord. My brother will be there and my grandparents. It should be a good time. I'll be back the following Monday."

"That sounds like fun. Hopefully, the weather will cooperate. It's not fun when the boats stop running. But usually, unless it's really bad, you should be able to get a flight out."

Alex made a face. "I'm actually not a fan of flying, especially those small planes that come here."

"You'll probably be fine. Just keep an eye on the weather. How are you settling in? Have you had a chance to see much of the island yet?"

He laughed. "Yes. I've been going out with a few of the guys in the office almost every night. We've closed a few of the bars downtown. That makes it rough the next morning, but it's been fun."

"Ugh, I don't know how you can get up so early after being out late. I would have a hard time with that."

He grinned. "I'm used to it now. 'Work hard, play hard' is our motto in the office."

Gina glanced at the time. "Well, this has been fun. I should probably start walking over to the restaurant. It's getting late."

"I'll walk you over."

Five minutes later, they reached the entrance to Mimi's Place, and Alex pulled her in for a hug and surprised her with a quick kiss goodbye.

"I'll see you next Friday for the party. Do you want to swing by to get me around six thirty?"

"Sure, see you then."

"Do you think he'll take it? I could see if they might be able to do a sign-on bonus, but I don't want to do that unless we know he's a lock, if he really wants it. Okay, call me on Monday." Billy put his phone down and ran a hand through his hair, which was already mussed up and going in different directions.

"Is it Colby? Did they come in with a low offer?" Jill asked. She guessed by the conversation that Billy was talking about his search at Colby Financial. They were a good client, but their salaries tended to be a little below market, which made closing candidates on their jobs challenging. It was unusual that Billy would take a business call on a Saturday, but Eric was one of their newer recruiters. He hadn't heard back from his candidate by end of the day on Friday, so when he finally did, he called Billy, nervous that his deal was about to fall apart.

Billy nodded. "I don't think I can get the base salary up, but they might flex to do more on the bonus. They'll have to if they want to get the best candidates." He walked over, put his hands on Jill's shoulders, and began kneading the muscles there. Jill closed her eyes and relaxed. Billy gave the best neck and shoulder massages. They spent so much time on the phone in their business that their muscles often tightened up.

She opened her eyes and glanced out the

window at the ocean. It was windy and the water was choppy with whitecapped waves. Mandy's house was close enough that they could faintly hear the sound of the surf hitting the sand. It was louder in the summer months when the windows were open. The house had a beautiful view, peaceful and relaxing.

"I have to admit, the pace here has been a nice change." Even though the restaurant got busy, it was a different kind of busy from their recruiting. When they were done with their shift at Mimi's, there was no work that went home with them. Still, Jill and Billy loved recruiting, and she knew by the time they went back after the New Year, they'd both be ready to get back in the office and be chaotically busy again. They both thrived on the energy and fast pace.

Billy sat on the edge of the bed, and Jill stood and started kneading his shoulders.

"It's been fun so far and great seeing your family," he said. "Mom called earlier while you were in the shower. I told her we'd head out to see them for our second Christmas the weekend after New Year's."

"That's perfect. I hope she's not too sad that we won't be there on Christmas Day." Jill felt bad about that, but it was impossible to see both families.

"When I told her that next year we'll spend it with them, she was fine with it."

"Good. And at least your brother and sister will be there."

Billy laughed. "Right. I told her she won't even miss us. She didn't think that was funny."

Mandy was on her way out when Jill and Billy arrived at the restaurant. She'd worked the lunch shift and was going out to dinner with Matt and his friend Kevin and his date.

"Whoever that is, he didn't say. I have no idea who Kevin's dating now. He's Matt's best friend, and he said he hasn't gone on a date in ages."

"Well, have fun," Jill said. "You can tell us all about it when we get home."

"Thanks. Here's the reservations book. We're steady, but there's room for some last-minute reservations or walk-ins." She turned it around so Billy and Emma, who had walked over, could see.

"Great, we're on it," Billy said.

Jill made her way over to the bar, where Gina had just arrived and was tying her apron around her waist. She helped Gina stock the bar for the night, made sure they had plenty of ice, changed a beer keg, and cut more fruit for garnishes.

Once they were all set, Jill poured herself a glass of water and leaned against the bar while Gina fished around in her apron for an elastic band and pulled her hair into a ponytail.

"So, how's it going with that guy you went on the date with? Mandy said you had a good time."

"With Alex? We did. We went to the movies this afternoon too, and next Friday I'm going to his company's Christmas party."

"Wow, so you really like this guy then?"

Gina hesitated. "I think so. It's not that big a deal going to his company party. I think he just needed a date and didn't want to go alone. I am curious to check out the place they are having it though. It's at the Whitley. Have you been there?"

Jill nodded. "Yes, Cory always has his Christmas parties there. It's very exclusive and expensive, and he likes everyone to know that. Mandy used to go every year, and she took me one year when I was visiting. I'm sure you'll have a great time. He pulls out all the stops."

"It's that fancy, huh? I might need to go shopping. I haven't worn a cocktail dress since I moved here and very rarely before that."

"That will be fun. I'd get a little black dress, something you can wear again. You can't go wrong with that. Or actually, with your hair, a red dress would be gorgeous."

Two older ladies came into the bar, and Jill went over to help them. They both ordered vodka martinis with a twist and the broiled scrod with Newburg sauce, which was on Paul's new prix fixe menu.

"Our friend Charlotte was in here last week, and she raved about these new specials you have. They are a great deal," one of the ladies said as Jill jotted down their order.

"I think so too," she agreed. "That comes with your choice of clam chowder or Caesar salad."

"Chowder for me."

"And salad for me," the other lady said.

Jill punched their order into the computer and went into the kitchen to get hot rolls and butter for them.

It was still early and not busy yet in the kitchen, so as Jill was filling a basket with rolls, she told Paul that her two customers came in because their friend loved the new menu and they both ordered from it too.

"That's good to hear. Tell them they're going to have a tough choice for dessert. Jared made a key lime crème brûlée that is fantastic, and we have a new flourless chocolate lava cake scented with orange. That's good too."

Jill's stomach rumbled. "I might need to try those…so I can accurately describe them to customers."

Paul laughed. "I'll make a sample tasting plate for you and Gina so you can both try. Hold on." He put a slice of the chocolate cake and a small round ramekin of the key lime crème brûlée on a plate and added a dollop of fresh whipped cream to both desserts. "Here you go."

"Thank you!" Jill took the plate of desserts and basket of rolls and headed back to the bar. They still only had the two ladies for customers at the bar, and after dropping their bread basket off, Jill pulled Gina into the nook behind the bar where they kept extra stock and where they couldn't be seen by customers, but where they could still see the front door and if anyone was coming toward the bar. She set the plate of desserts down. "This is from Paul. The two desserts that go with the prix fixe menu. Jared made this one."

Gina dipped a spoon into the crème brûlée, and a look of surprise came upon her face. "Oh, that is so good. It's like key lime pie, but better."

Jill liked the crème brûlée but loved the warm chocolate cake with its hint of orange flavor. They quickly ate most of the desserts and set them aside to finish later.

The bar started to fill up, and Jill and Gina were busy for the next hour. Gina had just served the two older ladies their desserts when one of them motioned toward the television. The news was on and there was another warning about the dangers of frozen pipes.

"That poor family. Imagine having to move out of your home right before the holidays. Insurance should cover most of the repair costs, but I heard she lost all the gifts she'd bought and wrapped. She was all done shopping!" one of them said.

The other lady smiled. "Well, I just heard that someone made a big donation. They called and asked for a list of the items she lost—the gifts. And they went shopping, wrapped everything, and dropped off two big garbage bags worth of gifts at their hotel's front desk."

"Who did that? Do they know?"

The older woman shook her head. "No idea. She wanted to be anonymous, I guess. All I know is that she had white hair, like us!"

"It wasn't me," the other lady said, and her friend laughed.

"No, wasn't me either. I can't afford to do that. But bless her heart, whoever it was."

———

Matt and Mandy were meeting Kevin and his date at the Gaslight at seven. The plan was to have dinner and stay and listen to some live music. The Gaslight was right downtown and had an intriguing menu, with lots of small plates and creative appetizers. Mandy loved their tuna nachos.

When they reached the front door of the restaurant, they spotted Kevin coming their way with his date, and both Mandy's and Matt's jaws dropped. Matt turned to Mandy and lowered his voice. "I had no idea, I swear. Kevin told me that he met someone a week or so ago at happy hour. He did say her name was Amy, but I never made the connection. I was kind of distracted at the time and didn't ask any questions. I guess I should have."

Mandy took a breath. At least if Amy was dating Kevin, maybe she'd stop flirting with Matt. So, it might not be a bad thing—though she wasn't keen to spend an evening with the other woman.

Kevin looked happy though, and Amy was all smiles as she walked along with her arm through his.

"I'm glad we could all do this tonight," Kevin said. He glanced at Amy, and it was clear that he was smitten. "Matt, Mandy, I'd like you to meet Amy."

"We met recently, at the Crosswinds," Amy said. "And I know Matt from the Nantucket Boat Basin."

"It's nice to see you again," Mandy said politely.

Matt nodded. "Kevin mentioned he was dating someone new. I didn't realize that it was you, Amy."

Amy grinned. "When Kevin told me you were one of his best friends, I took it as a sign."

Kevin looked confused. "You didn't say anything. I didn't know you knew each other."

"Didn't I? Sorry about that. I meant to." She smiled at him, and he melted.

"Shall we go in?" Matt suggested.

They were seated at a cozy table near a fireplace that was filled with candles. Amy and Kevin sat next to each other on a bench, and Mandy and Matt were opposite them on chairs. They ordered cocktails: white wine for Mandy, vodka and soda for Amy, and beers for the guys. They decided on a bunch of appetizers, including tuna nachos and small plates of braised short ribs and fried chicken sliders.

The conversation was…interesting. Kevin was mostly silent and Amy talked nonstop. By the time they finished eating, Mandy had learned more than she ever wanted to know about Kevin's new girl-friend. She was surprised to learn that Amy was older than she'd thought. She'd recently turned forty.

Tonight, she was wearing high heels, skinny jeans, and a powder-blue sweater. Up close though, Mandy could see that Amy wore more makeup than she'd realized when she first met her. She was also pretty sure that Amy was wearing false eyelashes, which seemed to be all the rage with some women. Mandy couldn't imagine bothering with that. She was fine with the same mascara she'd been using since she was in high school. It was Maybelline, very black, and in a pink and green tube. It did the job just fine.

She realized, too, that when Amy shook her head, her hair didn't move. It was fluffed and sprayed to death. It was a flattering cut though, and it made her brown eyes look bigger.

"How did you two meet?" Amy asked Mandy at one point.

"At the restaurant where I work. Matt came in often, and we got to chatting."

Matt grinned. "I wanted to ask her out for months, but she wasn't interested in dating for a while."

"Oh, right. You were married to Cory Lawson. I used to see him out at the Club Car all the time. That's where I met Kevin too."

Mandy just nodded. She hadn't realized it at the time, but many of the nights when Cory said he was working late, he was actually playing late, out with the young guys in his office or with one of his many women "friends."

"He's a good-looking guy, and they say he's one of the wealthiest men on Nantucket. I'm not sure I would have let him go—though I imagine you did okay in the divorce."

Mandy was speechless. She wasn't sure how to respond to that. It was none of Amy's business.

Matt spoke up and changed the subject. "Here comes our waitress. Does anyone want another drink? I think the music is about to start."

"I'd love another wine." Mandy was eager for the music to start so that she wouldn't have to talk to Amy.

"I'll have another too. Thanks, Matt." Amy turned her megawatt smile on him, but Matt missed it because he was leaning over to give Mandy a quick kiss. He whispered softly. "I am so sorry about this. We don't have to stay long. Want to leave after the first set?"

She nodded. "It's not your fault. And that sounds perfect."

The band was good, and they all enjoyed the music. It was loud enough that conversation was difficult, so they just relaxed and listened to the band. At the end of the first set, Matt pulled out his wallet and set some cash down on the table.

"This was fun, but I think we're going to get going. Mandy and I both have to be up early tomorrow."

"So soon?" Amy protested.

Kevin smiled at her. "It's okay. We can stay for

the next set." He turned back to Matt and Mandy. "This was fun. We'll have to do it again sometime."

Matt just nodded and Mandy stood and pulled on her coat. "Enjoy the next set," she said.

Once she and Matt were outside, Mandy laughed. "Well, that was quite the evening. Your friend Kevin really seems to like her though."

"He does. I wish them both well, but I'm in no hurry to do this again."

10

Gina was wiping down the kitchen counter when she heard footsteps outside the door, followed by a knock. She opened the door to let Jared in. They were heading over to the Festival of Trees.

He stepped in, stopped, and sniffed the air. "Smells like cookies. Were you baking?"

She smiled. "Yes, I just made my Christmas pizzelles. I make a big batch every year. It's a family tradition."

"I'm not familiar with those. What are they like?"

"Try one." Gina walked over to one of the stacks of cookies. They were wafer-thin, dusted with powdered sugar, and looked like delicate snow-flakes. She lifted one and placed it on a paper towel so it wouldn't shake sugar on him. "If you like it, I'll give you some to take with you. As you can see, the recipe makes a lot."

Jared took a bite as he looked around the kitchen at the piles of the cookies on paper towels all across the counter.

"Oh, this is good. Is that anise?"

"Yes. It's the traditional Italian flavor. But some use lemon or vanilla instead. I like the anise. I'll wrap up a stack for you. They're great in the morning with coffee."

"What do you use to make them? Some kind of waffle press?"

"A pizzelle press. It's similar to a waffle machine and has the snowflake design etched in. They only take about a minute each to cook." She grabbed a handful of the cookies and wrapped them in a sheet of aluminum foil and handed it to him. "Here you go. I'll probably bring some into the restaurant too, so if you run out, there will be more there. I'm going to run and change this sweater to one without sugar. I'll be right back. Help yourself to another cookie."

"Thanks, I think I will."

Gina went off to put on a clean sweater, and when she returned, Jared was standing in her living room, looking at her easel with the half-finished painting. She had it set up by the big window that let in the best light.

"You did this?" He sounded surprised and impressed.

She nodded. "I went to school for art but got away from it. I haven't touched my brushes or paints in over a year, and they are in rough shape. My brushes really need to be replaced, but for now, I'm having fun." The picture was of one of her favorite holiday sights—the lighthouse at Brant Point decorated for Christmas with a big red ribbon. She had a photo that she was using for inspiration, and it wasn't coming out too badly, so far. She thought she'd be rusty, but painting seemed to be coming right back to her.

"That's really good. You're talented." He grinned. "I can barely manage stick people."

"Thanks! Well, I'm ready if you are. Don't forget your cookies."

They decided to walk as it wasn't too far and the sun was shining. It was cold but overall a nice, clear day.

"I know you said you haven't been to the Festival of Trees, but have you been to the Whaling Museum yet?" Jared asked.

"No. I heard it's good though. I've meant to go but haven't made it over there yet."

"Good, you'll like it. There's a lot to see, and it will be even more fun with the trees."

There was a small line when they arrived, but it moved quickly, and soon they were inside. The inside of the museum was like a winter wonderland with decorated trees everywhere. They roamed around looking at all of them. Each had its own personality, depending on who had decorated it—local businesses, children, artists. They were all beautiful.

When they finished looking at the trees, Jared showed her around the rest of the museum, which was more interesting than Gina had expected. It was probably partly due to Jared's commentary as they went along. She discovered that he was a big reader. Dennis Lehane was his favorite author, and it turned out they'd gone to the same private Catholic school in Boston, BC High, though Dennis graduated almost twenty years before Jared did. He was also a history buff.

"Did you know that they say in five hundred years, Nantucket won't be here? It will be underwater."

"That's a scary thought."

"I know, right?"

They looked at beautifully decorated scrimshaw pieces—whale teeth that had designs etched into them—and there was a whole section with clothing worn in historic times. They were at the museum for over two hours, and the time went by so fast.

They got back to Gina's place around three thirty—just in time for her to change for work and head in. Jared was about to jump in his car and do the same: stop home and then go into work.

He paused before getting into his car. "Thanks for the cookies. I had fun today."

She smiled. "I did too. Thanks for showing me the Festival of Trees. I think I might have to get a tree this week, maybe. I didn't do it last year, and I like the way it makes my living room feel so bright and cheery."

"Are you going to get a real tree?"

"Of course! I'm not a fan of the fake ones."

"I'm not either." He glanced at Gina's Jetta. "You won't be able to get it home in that though. We can use my Jeep. I think we're both off on Tuesday. We could go then?"

"Sure, if it's not too much trouble, that would be great."

"It's no trouble at all. I know just where to go. I got my mom's tree yesterday at Bartlett's Farm. We could grab dinner after and maybe play some trivia. It's Christmas trivia this week; should be fun."

"You like trivia? I used to play in Boston with some friends all the time. I miss it."

"Yeah, I like trivia. I usually do okay with the history and geography questions."

Gina laughed. "Good, because those are my weakness. For some reason, I do okay with science ones and entertainment, movies, books."

"So, we'll make a good team then. It will be fun."

She smiled. "I'm looking forward to it. See you in a bit." Gina went inside and turned on the radio, which was playing Christmas carols. She found herself humming along as she wrapped the cooled stacks of cookies in foil to keep them fresh. Boots came running to greet her and rubbed against her legs, purring loudly. Gina scooped her up and gave her a hug.

"I love that you're so happy to see me. But I really wasn't gone long!" She glanced at Boots's food bowl and laughed. "Right, you're just hungry. That makes more sense." She filled the bowl with food before going to change for work. Once again, she'd had a really good time with Jared and couldn't help comparing him to Alex. They were both handsome in their own ways, but very different personality-wise. Alex was a go-getter: extroverted, energetic, and successful.

And Jared was quieter, but she was beginning to see that he was equally passionate about the things he cared about. And he was a lot of fun and easy to be with, but it was comfortable, like time spent with a good friend, while Alex was maybe a little more exciting. But was that what she wanted?

11

"Don't forget your mittens!" Jill called as Billy opened the front door. Matt had just pulled up, and the two men were heading off to go ice fishing for the afternoon.

Billy laughed, came back inside, and gratefully took the black leather gloves that Jill was holding up.

"Thanks, and they're not mittens. Men don't wear mittens."

"Whatever! Have fun, you guys."

"If you catch a fish, we'll cook it up for dinner tonight," Mandy added.

Soon after Billy left, Mandy and Jill left as well

for the Hodgeses' holiday open house. It was Cory's weekend with the kids, so just Jill and Mandy were going.

"I feel bad that Emma can't join us," Jill said as Mandy pulled up to the Beach Plum Cove Inn.

"I don't think she minds. She and Paul like working a double together on Sunday and then having Monday off."

It was a few minutes past noon, and there was already a good crowd gathered. Cars were parked all up and down the street. They found a spot, and Mandy grabbed the bottle of wine she'd wrapped in gold foil and red ribbon to give to Lisa from the two of them as a hostess gift. The house was decorated beautifully with twinkling white lights outside and in, red velvet bows on the bushes, and a gorgeous wreath on the front door made of driftwood that had been painted pale blue with pretty seashells wired onto it and a crinkly silver ribbon.

"I bet Lisa made that," Mandy said. "Kate told me her mother always makes a holiday wreath."

Jill knocked on the front door, and a moment later it was opened by Lisa's husband, Rhett, who was wearing a big smile and a shimmering red holiday vest over a hunter-green button-down shirt.

"Welcome! Come in." He opened the door wide, and they stepped inside. Mandy handed him the bottle of wine.

"You look festive. I love the vest," Jill said.

"Thank you. It's a tradition. I've worn this every holiday for years."

Lisa saw them and came over to say hello. "We call it his Festivus vest," she said.

Mandy and Jill laughed. "That was one of my favorite *Seinfeld* episodes," Mandy said.

"'A Festivus for the rest of us,'" Jill said and they all laughed.

"Exactly. Come on in and help yourself to the food. It's in the dining room and the kitchen," Lisa said.

"And there's tons, so eat up," Rhett added.

"Kate told me that you're back for the whole

month of December, Jill. That's wonderful," Lisa said. "Have you seen Natalie yet? She's getting so big."

"No, not yet. Just Abby and Kate so far."

"You made it!" Kate walked over and gave them both a hug. "Let me make you both a mimosa. I can't have one, but you both might as well."

Mandy raised her eyebrows. "You always have a mimosa. Are you…?"

Kate grinned. "Yes, three months along as of today, so Jack gave me the green light to tell everyone. In another month or so, we'll find out what we're having."

Mandy hugged her again. "Kate, I'm so happy for you."

"Me too. That's great news," Jill added. She noticed that Kate was positively glowing. Her hair was shinier than usual, and she had a new rosy tone to her cheeks. And she was still as slim as ever. She expected Kate would be one of the people who didn't show until month five and was all baby, slim everywhere else but with a basketball in her belly. She smiled at the image.

"Have you had any cravings yet?" Mandy asked her.

Kate laughed. "Yes, and it's the strangest thing. I used to love coffee, but now I can't stand the smell of it, and instead I'm drinking tea with milk. I never put milk in anything before. And potato chips. I can't get enough of them and I know they are awful for you. But they keep finding their way into every sandwich I make, an actual layer of chips on top of whatever else—turkey, ham, even peanut butter. I know that's super weird, but it's so good."

"It's not weird. I had my share of strange cravings too," Mandy assured her. "Some of them stayed with me. I still crave fried clams every now and then."

"Well, I crave those, and I've never been pregnant. They're just really good," Jill said.

"Speaking of really good, here are your mimosas." Kate handed them each a tall champagne flute filled with champagne and fresh-squeezed orange juice. "And grab a plate and eat. My mother went overboard, as usual. She's always afraid that she won't have enough food."

Mandy and Jill each reached for a plump shrimp, dunked it in cocktail sauce, and followed Kate into the dining room, where platters of food were everywhere. They made their way around the room, adding stuffed mushrooms, various dips and chips, a small wedge of Lisa's famous lobster quiche, and a bite-sized chunk of lobster tail. The lobster pieces had toothpicks in them, and a small pot of melted butter nearby was set over a candle to keep it warm. They dipped the lobster in the butter before taking a bite.

"I think this may be my favorite appetizer of all time," Mandy said.

"It's so simple too," Kate said. "Jack brought the lobster tails home from work, and we just chopped them up and melted some butter."

"I'll have to remember that for when Billy and I have people over when we're back in Manhattan. It's an impressive dish."

They saved room for the cinnamon walnut coffee cake that Lisa always made. It had sour cream in it and was the moistest, most decadent coffee cake. And it went really well with the mimosas.

Kate wandered off to mingle with other guests, and after they finished eating, Mandy and Jill took their barely touched mimosas into the living room, where a giant, beautifully decorated tree stood in the corner and Rhett was sitting at the piano playing Christmas carols. Abby waved to them to come join her on the sofa where she was sitting with her daughter, Natalie, who was about two and half, if Jill remembered right. The girl did look much bigger than the last time Jill had seen her. She was very cute in her red velvet holiday dress with smocking details at the top and black patent-leather Mary Jane shoes and white socks. Her soft baby curls were tied back with a black velvet ribbon. In her lap, she had a hardcover children's book with a picture of Elmo on the cover.

Jill and Mandy joined them on the sofa with Jill

sitting next to Natalie. Mandy smiled as she looked at Natalie's book. "My kids loved Elmo too."

"Natalie is obsessed with Elmo. She has a stuffed Elmo that goes with her everywhere."

Natalie's eyes filled up. "Where's my Elmo?" She looked all around them in a panic. But Abby calmly reached to her other side and pulled out the stuffed toy and handed it to her. "We moved him out of the way so you could read the book."

Natalie grabbed the Elmo toy and hugged it to her fiercely, then turned to Jill and handed her the book. "Read."

Mandy laughed. "She wants you to read to her."

"You don't have to," Abby said. "Natalie, we can read later, honey."

The little girl's eyes filled up with tears again, and she kissed the top of Elmo's head. Jill felt something shift inside her, a need to make those tears go away.

"I don't mind. I'm happy to read about Elmo."

"Natalie, you remember Jill? Say thank you."

"Thank you." Her eyes grew wide and dreamy

as Jill opened the book and started reading. A few minutes later, Natalie snuggled against her, and Jill got a whiff of baby shampoo. She kept reading and was almost done when Abby said, "You can stop. I think she's asleep."

Jill paused for a moment, and Natalie stirred and mumbled sleepily, "More."

Abby chuckled. "I guess I was wrong."

Jill kept reading, and five minutes later, the adventures of Elmo were over and Natalie was fast asleep.

"I should put her in my mother's bedroom and let her have a good nap." Abby stood, and Jill did the same, carefully lifting Natalie to pass her to her mother, but the little girl snuggled into the crook of her neck and clung on tight.

"Aw, she really likes you," Abby said.

And Jill was feeling something too, a maternal instinct that she'd secretly worried might be lacking. "I'll carry her there, if you show me where to go. Maybe she'll stay asleep."

"Sure, follow me."

Jill held on tight to the little girl so she wouldn't slip out of her grasp and followed Abby to Lisa and Rhett's bedroom, where there was a pink crib in the corner for when Natalie came to visit. Jill carefully set her down, and Abby covered her with a soft baby throw. Natalie murmured for a moment, then rolled to her side and let out a sigh.

"Okay, I think she's good for a while. Thanks for your help."

"It was nothing."

"I used to hate this question, so feel free to tell me to mind my own business, but you were really good with her. Are you and Billy planning to have kids soon?" Abby asked.

"If it was up to Billy, I'd already be expecting. But we haven't been married all that long. I didn't want to rush into having kids."

Abby nodded. "That makes sense. It was different for us because it took so long. Neither one of us expected that."

"I never thought about that." Jill hadn't given much thought at all to getting pregnant, other than she was in no hurry to do it. She wondered how it would be for her and Billy, and if it would take them a while too. And for the first time, she wondered what a mini Billy or a little girl like Natalie might look like.

12

Sunday afternoon was busier than usual at Mimi's Place. They always had a good crowd that came after church, and with Christmas right around the corner, there were probably people out shopping too. Emma glanced around the crowded dining room and noticed that Connie Boyle and her three friends were sitting with empty plates. She went over to help clear them out of the way.

"How was everything, ladies?" Emma asked as she gathered up their plates.

"As good as always, dear. Thank you," Connie said, and the other ladies nodded in agreement.

Emma brought the plates into the kitchen and unloaded them at the dishwasher station. She noticed that Stacy, the waitress serving Connie's table, was picking up a big order for another party.

"Stacy, I just cleared Connie's table. I'll check and see if they want anything else."

Stacy nodded. "Thank you. It will be a few minutes before I can get back to them."

"No worries." Emma walked back to the table. The ladies were in the middle of a conversation, so she waited for them to finish before interrupting.

"I heard the freezer broke at the food pantry. They are getting their shipment of turkeys on Tuesday for the Christmas baskets and don't know what they are going to do," one of the ladies said.

"Sounds like they need to fix that freezer fast or get a new one," Connie said.

"They do," the woman across from her said. "But it's so old that it's not worth fixing and a new one costs thousands that they don't have."

"Ladies, would you like coffee or tea?" Emma asked. "Or dessert?"

No one wanted dessert, but everyone wanted decaf coffee. Emma went off to get it, and when she returned, Connie was looking at her curiously.

"You have a big freezer here, Emma, right? What do they call it, a walk into or something like that?"

Emma realized what Connie was suggesting and thought it was a great idea. "A walk-in. Let me go check with Paul and see how much free room we have."

She went into the kitchen, found Paul behind the line pouring béarnaise sauce over a filet, and told him about the food pantry's broken freezer. He went into the walk-in and returned a moment later.

"We have room for about sixty turkeys. If they want to store them here, that's fine. I can meet them here on Tuesday before we open."

"Wonderful. I'll let Connie know."

Connie was thrilled with the news. "I'll call them

as soon as I get home. The delivery usually comes around nine. Will someone be here that early?"

"We'll make sure someone is here," Emma assured her.

Emma and Paul finished up around eight. Gina was closing the dining room and bar, and Jared was doing the same in the kitchen. Sunday nights tended to be slow, but Emma and Paul often stayed through the main dinner rush before leaving. They usually had a late dinner together once they got home, then stayed up late relaxing and watching a movie since they both had the next day off and could sleep in.

They rarely felt like cooking after spending the day at the restaurant and instead picked up Thai takeout or pizza, depending on their mood. But today, Paul surprised her.

"How does a good steak sound to you? That won't take too long."

"Sure, as long as you don't mind cooking."

He smiled. "I don't mind."

When they got home, Emma offered to help, but he shooed her away, so she decided to take a hot shower and wash off the feel of the restaurant. The hot water felt wonderful, and she took her time letting it wash over her. She changed into a pair of comfy sweats and a big oversized sweatshirt that was faded and soft from many washings. With still-damp hair, she padded into the kitchen and breathed deeply.

"That's not just steak. What else are you making? It smells heavenly."

Paul finished pouring a really good bottle of cabernet, so good that Emma raised her eyebrows as he handed her a glass. Most of the time, they drank good but inexpensive wine like a Josh cabernet, or even occasionally Paul picked up a box of wine, which they'd discovered was actually pretty good and stayed fresh longer than a bottle. This was one of the more expensive special blends from Charles Krug.

"I opened it when you got in the shower to give it a little time to breathe."

Emma took a sip. It was rich and smooth and made her taste buds very happy.

"This is delicious, but it seems a bit of a splurge for a Sunday night. I thought we were saving it for a special occasion. Not that I mind. I don't."

He laughed. "Well, it is a Sunday, but I hope it might be a special occasion." He took a quick sip, then set his wineglass on the counter and got down on one knee, surprising Emma totally.

"Paul, what are you doing?" She knew this was coming eventually, but she didn't expect it that night. Emma had wondered about maybe Christmas or New Year's Eve, though she had made it clear that she wasn't in any hurry.

"I'm trying to make this day special. I thought about giving this to you on Christmas or New Year's Eve, but then I realized what I love most about you—about us—is the little moments: spending our days and nights together doing ordinary things, relaxing with the cats, working together, laughing, and loving each other. I don't want to do this on a holiday. I just want you to know how special you are to me every day.

"I love you, Emma, and I love our life together, and I'd really love to make it official. We don't have to commit to a date, but I do want to commit to each other, and I hope you do too. Will you make me the happiest man on Nantucket and say you'll marry me?" He pulled a small box out of his pocket and opened it. The ring inside was perfect. It was a lovely diamond, not too big but not small, and it was set in an antique platinum setting. It was delicate and very pretty. "This was my grandmother's ring. If you don't like it, we can change it and get whatever you want."

Emma's eyes were suddenly watery, the ring blurry as she blinked back happy tears. "Yes! It's perfect, Paul. I love it. More importantly, I love you. Thank you for making this such a special Sunday."

He slid the ring on her finger, then stood and

pulled her in for a hug and a sweet kiss. They broke apart when the stove timer beeped.

"Dinner's ready. I hope you're hungry."

"I'm starving." She watched as Paul opened the oven and pulled out a pan containing two thick strip steaks smothered in a blue cheese and panko crumb topping that was browned from the broiler. He put each steak on a plate, then poured a red-wine reduction sauce over it and added scalloped potatoes and roasted asparagus.

"That looks amazing. I didn't realize we had any really good steaks." When he'd said "steak," she'd been picturing a simple thin cut, not these prime strips that were over an inch thick.

"I bought them yesterday and hid them in a drawer."

She admired his planning and couldn't wait to show her sisters the ring. They were going to be thrilled. They'd been waiting for this to happen almost since they all started working together. Emma knew both of her sisters had hoped that she and Paul would find their way back to each other. And they had. After going their separate ways after high school and marrying other people, they were back together, and it felt right. Emma sighed with contentment and couldn't stop staring at her ring. She was glad that Paul hadn't waited. He was right. Getting engaged at home on a Sunday night was much more special. It was perfect.

———

Mandy and Jill were drinking coffee in the kitchen Monday morning around nine when there was a knock on the door. Mandy glanced out the window and saw Emma's car parked out front. She often stopped in to visit over coffee on her day off, so Mandy didn't think anything of it. She opened the door as Emma was walking toward it.

"Perfect timing. I just made a fresh pot of coffee. Jill and I were just gabbing, and we have chocolate doughnuts too, if you're interested. I know we shouldn't, but I was hungry when I was at the store and couldn't help myself." Mandy stopped talking when Emma held up her hand and showed off the sparkly new engagement ring.

"Oh my gosh! And here I am babbling on about doughnuts. Come in, let me take a closer look."

Emma stepped inside, and Mandy took her hand and leaned in to admire the ring. "Em, it's really lovely. Congratulations."

"Thank you. It was his grandmother's."

They went in the kitchen, where Jill was already standing, and she came over to see the ring too.

"It's beautiful. When did he do it? Sit down and tell us everything."

Mandy poured Emma a cup of coffee and put a doughnut on a plate. Emma reached for it immediately and broke a piece off and popped it in her mouth. She loved sweets.

"He asked me last night. Made an amazing dinner while I was in the shower and then got down on one knee. It was a total surprise."

"I thought he might do it on Christmas," Jill said.

"I wondered about that too," Emma admitted. "But he said he didn't want to do it on a holiday. That it was special enough, just getting engaged, and Sunday night felt right."

"That's so romantic," Mandy said. "I'm so happy for you, Emma. Paul's such a great guy."

Emma smiled. "Thanks. I think so too."

"What are you two up to today?" Jill asked.

"We're heading off-island soon to do some shopping in Hyannis, and depending how much time we have, we might see a movie."

"That sounds like fun."

"We're probably stopping at Trader Joe's too, if you need anything."

"The cheddar!" Mandy and Jill said at the same time. They both loved a cheddar there that had a unique parmesan flavor.

Emma laughed. "Got it. Oh, by the way, just FYI, Paul and Jared are going in early tomorrow. We're boarding some frozen turkeys for a week or so." She told them about the food pantry's broken freezer.

"Oh, that's terrible timing for them." Mandy smiled. "Now I know what Abby was talking about. She texted me 'thank you' this morning. Now it makes sense." Abby was one of the main volunteers at the food pantry.

"Paul said there's plenty of room, so we were happy to help. It was actually Connie's idea."

"Is she involved with the food pantry?" Jill asked.

"I think she and a few of her friends help out occasionally, handing out the baskets on holidays like this," Mandy said.

"She seems to know all the gossip on Nantucket," Emma said as she reached for her last bit of doughnut.

"Any idea what a new freezer costs?" Mandy asked.

"The ladies with Connie said they are expensive, thousands of dollars."

Mandy nodded. "That's hard to come up with for a charity organization like that. I'm glad we had room in the walk-in."

"All right, I'm off. Thanks for the coffee. Tell Billy I said hello. Is he still sleeping?"

Jill laughed. "He's been up since six and on the phone for the last hour. He got a new search in yesterday."

"Oh, that's right. I forgot you're both doing some work remotely," Emma said.

"Billy is more than I am. I have a few of the associates handling some of my clients and candidates while I'm out. It's good experience for them, and it gives me a break. There are a few things I am still following up on, but it's been nice being able to relax and just enjoy working in the restaurant."

"We'll miss you both when you go back. You should do this again over the summer," Mandy suggested.

"I'd love to. I'll have to work on Billy, but I think I can get him to come around."

13

Jared came by Gina's cottage at four o'clock sharp. She heard his Jeep pull in and met him outside, hopping in the passenger seat for the drive out to Bartlett's Farm to pick out a tree. They had a good selection, and it didn't take long for Gina to choose one that she liked. She went with a Douglas fir, and Jared put it in the back of the Jeep and tied it down with a bungee cord.

When they got back to Gina's, he carried it inside, and she helped him get it placed into the stand. Once it was locked in, they stepped back to admire the tree. It was a beauty. Boots sat on the coffee table, watching them. Gina reached into a paper shopping bag and rummaged around until she found what she was looking for: the angel topper.

"Could you please reach up and put this on top?"

"Of course." Jared took the angel and easily secured it on the top of the tree.

"What about the rest? Do you want some help getting the ornaments on? The tree looks pretty naked," Jared said.

"I'd love that. I didn't want to bother you."

"I don't mind, and we have plenty of time still before dinner and trivia."

They spent the next hour decorating the tree, hanging all the many ornaments that Gina had collected over the years. Jared strung the white lights around the tree and connected the end to the angel, so that when all the ornaments were on, Gina flipped the switch, and the whole tree and the angel glowed merrily.

"We did well," Jared said, and Gina had to agree.

The room looked festive now because of the bright and cheery tree.

Jared drove them to the Rose and Crown, the pub-restaurant where they were going to have dinner and play trivia.

There was a good crowd for trivia night, and the dining room was full, but they found two seats at the bar and both decided to get burgers. Gina sipped a cabernet while they waited, and Jared had a draft IPA. When he lifted his glass, she noticed a deep scratch on his hand.

"Did you do that getting the tree?" She felt bad that he might have hurt himself helping her.

He shook his head. "No, it's from this morning. Paul and I went over to the restaurant to help carry in some cases of turkeys." He explained about the food pantry and the broken freezer. "A box slipped and a sharp edge got me. It's no big deal."

Their burgers arrived soon after, and as they were eating, the trivia host came around to give them pencils and paper and asked them what their team name was.

"I hadn't thought about that. What should we call ourselves?" Jared asked.

Gina thought for a moment. "Well, we both work at Mimi's Place, so let's go with that?"

"Sounds good."

They finished eating just as trivia began, and the theme for the week was Christmas. There were close to twenty teams playing, some with just one or two people and others with large groups of eight or more. Gina had played before with large teams. It was always fun but didn't necessarily give an advantage when people didn't agree on an answer.

"Okay everyone, here's our first question… In the TV special *How the Grinch Stole Christmas*, what three words best describe the Grinch?"

Jared stared at Gina, who was drawing a total blank. She knew this. She'd seen the movie a million times.

Jared's eyes lit up. "Stink…"

"Stank, stunk!" Gina said and laughed. As soon as he said the first word, the others came to her. They turned their answer in and were happy when the host announced the answer. But, based on the cheers going up around them, she guessed that most teams got it right. The games usually started out with an easy question.

It was fun playing with Jared because they usually either agreed or one of them knew the right answer easily when the other had no idea at all, so it balanced out. They were doing really well, and coming into the last question, they were in third place overall.

The trivia host addressed the room. "Okay, for the final question I need your wagers—remember, this time you can wager up to your total points if you wish." They thought about it and decided to wager all but two points, so if the question was really hard and everyone missed it, they'd still have a few points. Jared wrote their wager down and brought the slip of paper to the host.

Although they were in third place, Gina knew how easy it was to miss the last question and lose everything. The final question was rarely easy.

"Okay, here we go. In the holiday movie *A Christmas Story*, what was the name of the next-door neighbors whose dogs ate the Christmas turkey?"

"Oh, I'm no help at all," Gina said. "Would you believe that's the one Christmas movie I haven't seen?"

"My mother and I watch it every year and I'm still not sure. I want to say the Kravitzes, but I'm not one hundred percent sure."

"Well, they say you should always go with your first answer."

"Part of me is sure that's the name of the neighbors but something about it seems off. I don't know."

"Turn it in and we'll see." The top three teams would win Rose and Crown gift cards, which was always nice as they could use it on their next visit.

"Okay, everyone, here's your final answer. The next-door neighbors in *A Christmas Story* are not the Kravitzes. A few of you said that. That's from *Bewitched*, by the way. The correct answer is the Bumpuses."

Jared groaned along with most of the room.

"Only two teams got it right. So, remaining in third place, with two points—Mimi's Place!"

"Excellent!" Jared high-fived her and went up to collect their gift card.

The bartender dropped off their bill, and Jared threw a credit card down and handed it to him before Gina could even open her wallet.

"Are you sure? We can split it," she protested. She hoped he didn't think she expected him to pay for both of them.

He handed her the gift card. "Hold on to this, and we'll use it next time."

Gina tucked it in her wallet, and once Jared signed the slip, they left, along with most of the crowd that had been there for trivia.

"You were right by the way—your cookies were great with coffee. I polished off the last one this morning," Jared said when he pulled into her driveway.

"I love them for breakfast. I have tons more. Come on up and I'll give you some to take home."

"Sure. If you have plenty, I'll gladly take some off your hands."

They went inside, and Gina wrapped up a stack of cookies for Jared. She brought them over to where he was standing, admiring the tree. It looked beautiful, all decorated with the shimmering white lights.

"It really does look nice," she said.

"Beautiful," Jared said, but he wasn't looking at the tree anymore. His eyes met Gina's, and something shifted in the air between them. He leaned toward her, and she sucked in her breath, and then there was a loud crash and a howl as Boots toppled off the table beside the tree, taking the ornament that she was batting at with her.

They both laughed. "Well, I should probably get going," Jared said.

"Here's your cookies." She handed them to him.

"Thanks. I'm off this Friday. We could do something if you're off too, if you don't have plans?"

She hesitated. There was no doubt this time that Jared was asking her on a date, and she wanted to go, but she couldn't. Not this Friday.

"I'd love to. But I already have plans."

His face fell, the disappointment clear. "Oh, okay. Maybe another time soon then. I'll see you tomorrow at work."

"Good night, Jared."

14

"Mom, are you going to get married to Matt?"

Mandy set her coffee cup down and looked at her daughter, Brooke, who had a very serious and not happy expression. Blake chimed in with, "Are you going to have a baby too?"

Jill sat at the kitchen table with them, watching the scene unfold with interest. It was Wednesday morning, and Mandy and Jill were having coffee and making plans to head off-island to do some Christmas shopping. When Cory dropped the kids off the night before, after they'd gone out to dinner and watched a movie, it had been late. They were half asleep and ready for bed. Cory had simply smiled and waved from the car before driving off. She wanted to shake him. He'd blindsided her by news she suspected was coming, but it would have been nice to hear it first from Cory so they could have discussed how to share both the engagement and pregnancy with the kids.

"Matt is a really nice guy, and I'm enjoying his company. We haven't talked about getting married. If we do decide to do that, it won't be for a long time. And I don't have any intention of having another baby." She smiled. "I have my hands full with you two. Come here and give me a hug."

They did, and she hugged them both hard, then asked, "So, what exactly did your father say to you last night?"

"He was acting weird all day, weirder than usual," Brooke began. "He hired a horse and carriage to come to the house and take us downtown to some fancy restaurant. And then at dinner, he had a bottle of champagne delivered, and after the waiter opened it with a big pop, he got down on his knees! In the restaurant, with everyone looking. It was so embarrassing, Mom."

"And then he asked Hannah to marry him. And she said yes and started to cry," Blake said.

"And after all that, she didn't even have any champagne," Brooke added. "That's when Dad explained that she's having a baby. So, he drank almost the whole bottle of champagne himself. And then the carriage drove us home. Don't you think that's weird, Mom? I mean, she's really young, and Dad seems kind of old to have another baby."

Mandy tried not to laugh, because she agreed with her daughter. But, she was always careful not to be negative about Cory in front of them. "Your father seems very happy with Hannah, and it's not unusual for older men to marry younger women and start a new family. It doesn't mean he'll love you any less."

"Mom, we're not worried about that. We just think it's weird."

"Yeah," Blake agreed.

"Well, it is what it is. So, just make the best of it and be glad that your father is happy. On a different subject, I need your Christmas lists. Your aunt Jill and I are taking the ferry to Hyannis to do some shopping today."

They ran off to get their lists, and Jill shook her head. "Well, I suppose we knew that was coming. I didn't really see him getting married again so soon."

"I don't think he was planning on it," Mandy said dryly.

"Maybe he'll do a better job this time? Learn from his mistakes and all?"

Mandy wondered if he would. "I hope so, for her sake."

———

After they dropped the kids at school, Mandy and Jill took the fast ferry to Hyannis. Mandy was surprised by how crowded the boat was for the time of year, but guessed there were a lot of people out doing Christmas shopping too. They called for an Uber as the boat entered Hyannis Harbor and slowed the engines. As they disembarked, they saw their Uber vehicle pull up and, a few minutes later, were dropped at the Cape Cod Mall.

They had a good day of shopping, and Mandy was able to get through most of the kids' wish lists. They had lunch at Not Your Average Joe's, one of the few restaurants at the mall, and after they ate, they walked over to Barnes & Noble for coffee and book browsing.

"Have you thought about what to get Matt?" Jill asked as they sat in the café area and sipped their coffees.

"Lots of thoughts, but no idea what to get him. It's hard when he doesn't need a thing and we've only been dating for a few months."

"Yes, but you are pretty serious."

"Which makes it even more difficult. Any suggestions?"

Jill thought for a moment. "Does he have any interesting hobbies?"

"He loves fishing. But I'm sure he has everything he needs, and I wouldn't know what to look for anyway."

"Hmm. What about a coffee table book on fishing? Lots of big fish pictures? He might like that?"

"Maybe." Mandy wasn't convinced. A book didn't seem like enough.

"Well, you could get him something else too. Get him something you'd like to see him in. That's what I always do with Billy."

Mandy laughed. "That's not a bad idea. I did see a sweater in Nantucket Threads the other day that I thought would look great on him. It's a deep teal cashmere."

"There you go! Get that and the book, and you're done." Jill hesitated and said, "Unless you think he's going really BIG. Like an engagement ring?"

"We've only been dating a few months!" Mandy was shocked at the suggestion. Cory moved fast, but she didn't, and she was pretty sure that Matt didn't either. She couldn't imagine that a ring was even on his mind.

"Well, it hasn't been long for Cory either. Though she is pregnant."

"Right. Cory's situation is different. I think Matt and I are very much on the same page. I like the idea of a sweater. Do you want to help me find a book?"

"Sure, let's go."

15

Gina was starting to panic a little by lunchtime on Friday. Alex's company Christmas party was that night at the Whitley Hotel, and she still hadn't found a dress. She'd spent the morning going from shop to shop all over downtown Nantucket and just didn't love anything that she'd seen. There were some dresses that would have looked lovely, but their price tags were way out of her budget. That was one of the downsides of Nantucket—prices were higher than the norm because so many people that visited the island could easily afford them. She remembered when she first moved to Nantucket.

She'd been out window-shopping one day and stumbled into a shop that focused on cashmere sweaters—and the prices were sky-high.

Straight ahead was the Corner Table, where she loved to go sometimes for lunch or coffee. The food was delicious, and the atmosphere was casual and cozy. Her stomach rumbled, and she was tempted to stop in and take a break, but then she saw something in the window at Nantucket Threads that made her decide to hold on lunch and pop into Izzy's shop instead.

Izzy and her sister, Mia, sometimes came into the bar at Mimi's Place, and she'd gotten to know them a bit. She'd been into Izzy's store a bunch of times and loved it. Nantucket Threads was an eclectic mix of clothing, from touristy sweatshirts with *Nantucket* stamped across the front, to cute shorts and sweaters and other casual clothes. She didn't think she'd find dressier clothes, but she knew Izzy was always trying out new styles to see what might sell.

When she got closer to the shop, she paused outside to take a closer look at the window display and felt a happy thrill. There were two festive dresses, and they were both gorgeous. One was sleeveless black silk and cocktail length, and the other was a rich red jersey fabric with a boat neck and three-quarter-length sleeves. She loved both of them.

She stepped inside, and a moment later, Izzy came over to help.

"Gina, nice to see you! Are you looking for anything in particular?"

"I need a dress for a Christmas party tonight, actually. At the Whitley Hotel, so fancier than I would normally wear. I'd like to try both of the ones in your window, if possible."

"I just put those up today. It's a new designer. Come on back to the dressing room."

Gina followed Izzy to the back of the store.

"I'll be right back."

A moment later, she returned with two dresses and hung them up in the room for Gina.

"Let me know on the sizing. I'm usually pretty good at guessing by looking at someone, but see what you think."

Gina tried the black dress on first. It fit well and was flattering on. It was a basic black dress that she would definitely be able to wear again. She was relieved to finally find something that would work. And a glance at the price tag made her even happier. It was within her budget and lower than what she thought she'd end up paying on Nantucket. She appreciated that Izzy kept her prices reasonable so that year-round people could afford her clothes as well as the tourists.

"Let me see when you try each one on," Izzy called out.

Gina had been about to peel off the black dress and try on the red one, but instead she stepped out of the dressing room and twirled around so Izzy could see how the dress fit.

"That fits you perfectly. You're going to the Whitley?"

Gina nodded.

"Well, that should do there. I haven't been, but I hear it's lovely. Let's see how the red one looks."

Gina went back in the dressing room and carefully took off the dress and hung it back up. She slipped the red dress over her head and immediately liked the smooth feel of the material as it shimmied into place. She turned and looked in the mirror and smiled. It was a gorgeous dress, and the bright-red color felt really festive. She opened the dressing room door and let Izzy have a look.

"Well, that's it then. You have to get that dress. It looks amazing on you. The black one did too, but this one is really special. It's very flattering. What do you think?"

"I agree. I love it!"

Izzy packed up the dress, and Gina paid, then stopped at the Corner Table on her way home to get some soup to go. She could relax and take her time getting ready. She was starting to feel excited about going to the Whitley. Most people she knew had only heard about how exclusive and exquisite it was but had never actually gone there.

———

At six thirty, Gina stepped out of her bedroom, feeling confident in her new red dress. She slipped on a relatively comfortable pair of black patent-leather heels and found a matching small purse. A rustling sound got her attention. Boots was rolling around under the Christmas tree, trying to knock an ornament off a branch. She stopped that bad behavior by opening a can of food, and the cat came running.

Once Boots was fed, Gina stood for a moment and just stared at her tree. It looked magnificent. She'd added some wrapped gifts underneath that she'd be giving out to friends, and she still had some more shopping to do. She turned off the tree lights before leaving and pulled into Alex's driveway a few minutes later.

She was about to get out of the car when his

front door opened, and he came bounding out and hopped in the passenger side with a slightly sheepish look.

"Hey there, thanks for driving again. I think I am going to get a car. When I go home for Christmas, I'll see if I can pick something up and drive it back over on the slow boat. I didn't think I'd need one, but it will definitely be more convenient."

Gina agreed. "I like having a car here. I don't use it much, but it's nice to have it just in case."

"Are you excited about the party? The guys have been talking about it all week. Sounds like Cory really throws a big bash. And his partner is coming too. The whole Boston office is flying in and staying at the Whitley."

"Oh, is the Boston office big?"

"Similar size. There's about ten people in our office, including two assistants. And everyone is bringing their spouse or a date. Thanks again for agreeing to come with me."

"Of course. I have to admit I'm curious to see

this hotel. Hardly anyone I know has actually been there."

Fifteen minutes later, they pulled into a long, winding driveway that led to a sprawling resort that had a main white-shingled building surrounded by scattered cottages and sweeping lawns. In the distance, they could see the ocean and hear the unmistakable sound of surf crashing against the shore.

"The guys said there is valet parking, so just pull up to the front door."

Gina did as instructed and followed the circular driveway to the front door. A valet all in black with a sharp white cap rushed over to help. She handed him her keys, and she and Alex went inside.

The front doors were heavy glass. Two doormen stood by them and each opened a door as Gina and Alex approached. They stepped into the main lobby, which was breathtakingly elegant. The floors were white Carrara marble, and there were waterfall-style stone fountains and sky-high ceilings. The whole room was decorated for the holidays with giant red velvet ribbons and poinsettias everywhere, as well as oversized white candles nestled in a bed of seashells and surrounded by glass. It was all so lovely.

Alex led the way to the front desk, where a pretty woman with a sleek brown bob smiled.

"Welcome to the Whitley Hotel. How can I help you?"

"We're here for the Lawson Group's Christmas party," Alex said.

"Of course. Go straight down that hall and into the Oyster Room. Have a wonderful time."

They made their way to the Oyster Room, where a good crowd was already gathered. Stacy from the restaurant and her husband, John, waved when they saw them. They were standing by one of five big round tables.

"Let's go say hello to Stacy and John. Maybe we can sit with them," Gina suggested. She was glad to see a familiar face. She really liked Stacy and knew she rarely got out, since she was usually either working at the restaurant or home with her children.

"Sure. John's a good guy. I want to introduce you to everyone too."

They made their way over to Stacy and John's table.

"I'm so glad you're here," Stacy admitted.

"I just said the same to Alex." They chatted for a bit and then Alex wanted to mingle. "Can I set my purse next to you? We'll be back soon."

Alex led her first to the bar, which was set up in a corner of the room. "What would you like?"

"Chardonnay, please."

He ordered a Scotch on the rocks for himself.

"I didn't know you were a Scotch drinker." He'd had beer when they'd gone out before.

"I'm trying to acquire a taste for it. It's what a lot of these guys drink. It's not too bad. It grows on you."

They got their drinks, and Alex led her over to a sea of suits. The first person he introduced her to was Cory Lawson. She'd seen him before, of course. Everyone knew who Cory Lawson was. She'd waited on him at the bar a few times before he headed to a table where he usually ordered the most expensive things on the menu and always picked up the tab. He never brought a girlfriend in though, not since Mandy and her sisters took over the restaurant. So, as much of a jerk as she'd heard he was to Mandy, Gina was glad he never crossed that line of flaunting his dates there.

"Nice to meet you, Gina. I recognize you from Mimi's Place, of course. The food is wonderful there. I've always been a fan."

"It's very nice to meet you too." Gina noticed he was drinking Scotch too, and smiled. So, that's where Alex got it from.

"This is my fiancée, Hannah." Cory introduced her to his much younger girlfriend. Hannah was very pretty, but had a somewhat pained expression and didn't look like she was having a very good time. She also noticed that Hannah was the only person who didn't have a cocktail. And a moment later, she saw Hannah pat her stomach and whisper something to Cory before heading to the ladies' room.

"Hannah's a little under the weather," Cory said. "Morning sickness, but hers happens morning, noon, and night."

"Congratulations," Alex said.

Cory smiled. "Thanks. She just gave me permission to share the good news. We're both excited."

Gina wondered if Hannah was as excited as Cory. She hoped so. Hannah was very young, and they hadn't been dating all that long. She likely conceived early on since most people didn't share the news until the baby was about three months along.

Someone else came over to talk to Cory, and Alex introduced Gina to the rest of the people in the office. She met the two admins, who were lovely. There were several other analysts and two more senior-level guys, Jim and Todd, who were in the role that Alex aspired to. They were both portfolio managers. They had a swagger about them, and it was clear that they loved what they did. Alex's face lit up as they stood talking.

Their wives came over, each holding a glass of wine, and were introduced to Gina. Bethany and Jessica both had the upscale, preppy look that was so often seen on Nantucket. They were both blond, with razor-straight hair that fell to the tops of their shoulders and dresses that Gina had seen in the local shops and couldn't begin to afford.

They were friendly to Gina until one of them recognized her. "You work at Mimi's Place, right? In the bar." Her expression when she said "bar" looked as though she'd bitten into a sour lemon. Gina knew that look. It meant she'd just been dismissed as inferior.

She smiled proudly. "Yes, I manage the bar and sometimes the dining room."

"I worked in a restaurant one summer when I was in college. I hated it and swore never again," Bethany said.

Gina suspected that she probably wasn't very

good at it. Restaurant work could be challenging, and not everyone could keep up with the fast pace. Or had the right temperament for it.

"I knew better than to even try," Jessica said with a smile. "I think I'd be horrible at it." She seemed a little bit nicer, and Gina just smiled back in response.

"Do you want to go sit?" Bethany asked. Jessica nodded.

"Nice to meet you, Gina," Jessica said as the two of them turned to leave.

"We have room at our table, if you want to join us," Alex invited them.

"Sure, lead the way," Jim said.

Stacy looked up with interest when they all returned to the table. Introductions were made, and Bethany was unimpressed to learn that Stacy not only had three children but also waitressed at Mimi's Place with Gina. Jessica was polite though.

"That sounds like hard work, working at the restaurant and raising little children."

Stacy smiled. "It keeps me busy."

"Well, maybe if it works out with John, you won't have to work as much," Bethany said. "Neither of us work."

Gina couldn't imagine not working. "Don't you get bored?" she asked before she could stop herself.

Bethany laughed. "Hardly. We joined a ladies' golf league at the club and we're active with local charities. Cory's ex-wife Mandy used to do a lot of charity work with us, before the divorce. I hear she's working at your restaurant now. That's such a shame."

Gina had to keep from letting her temper show. "Mandy is one of the owners of that restaurant, and she told me she was dying of boredom and eager to work. She loves it there."

"Hmm. Well, good for her." Bethany lifted her glass toward the waiter to indicate that she wanted another. She turned to Jessica, and the two of them chatted, talking softly so that no one else could hear them.

Stacy leaned over and whispered to Gina, "She's

horrid. Poor Todd to be married to her. I know John said Todd is a great guy. All the guys are, it seems."

"Alex seems to really like it there."

A waiter carrying a silver tray with sweet broiled Nantucket scallops wrapped in bacon stopped by their table and everyone took a scallop or two. A moment later another tray came by, this time with puffy wonton chips topped with diced raw tuna mixed with chili oil, lemon, and avocado. More appetizers followed, and everything was exquisite.

"Oh, look what they just brought in," Todd said excitedly. "Come on, everyone, you have to try this. It's insane. Cory had the vodka and caviar bar last year too. Go easy though. I had five shots last year and didn't feel a thing, and then it suddenly hit me."

They all followed Todd over to the long side table that had elaborate ice sculptures, five different kinds of top-shelf vodka and bowls of caviar, miniature buttered toasts, and tiny blini pancakes, and toppings like minced onion, egg, and sour cream.

Gina had never tried caviar and watched Todd as he built the perfect caviar bite, with a little of everything on the buttered toast.

"So, first you pop this in your mouth and then you wash it down with an ice-cold vodka."

The attendant picked up the bottle of vodka that Todd selected, poured a shot into the ice luge, and collected the icy vodka at the bottom in a chilled shot glass.

"You have to try this," Alex said to Gina.

"I'm not much of a vodka drinker," she protested. "But the caviar looks interesting."

Todd overheard her and grinned.

"Trust me. You'll like vodka this way. Just try a small shot, ask for half the normal amount. They'll do that, right?" He glanced at the attendant who nodded.

Gina stepped up and put some caviar on toast the way she'd seen Todd do it, with a bit of onion, egg, and sour cream. She took a tentative bite, and it was much better than she expected, an explosion of slightly salty flavor. She finished it, accepted the half-size chilled vodka shot, and swallowed it quickly. And was surprised to find that Todd was absolutely right. If she wasn't driving, she would have been tempted to have another and maybe even a full shot. The vodka and caviar complemented each other and made everything taste better.

All the guys and Bethany and Jessica went through the line twice. Stacy had tried a smaller amount, like Gina, as she was also driving.

Gina thought they were done, but then Todd excitedly said, "One more shot!"

All the women went back to the table while the guys went through the line again for more vodka and caviar. They returned to the table a few minutes later and the talk quickly grew louder and looser as dollar amounts began flying around. Stacy and Gina glanced at each other.

"You two are lucky you landed here. You'll do well enough now, but in a few years, when you move into the PM role, you'll see what I mean." Todd glanced at Stacy. "You won't have to worry about working ever again, unless you want to."

"We just moved into a new waterfront house and paid cash. Todd's year-end bonus money," Bethany said.

"It was just north of two mil last year," Todd said proudly.

"And this year we did even better," Jim added. "We might come close to three, based on the numbers."

"Wow. That's incredible." Alex was in awe.

Todd grinned. "It doesn't suck. That will be you two someday, if you work hard."

Gina excused herself to use the ladies' room. When she was washing her hands, she heard a horrible wrenching sound, followed by what sounded like tears.

"Are you okay?" she asked. Whoever it was sounded deeply unhappy.

A moment later, the stall door opened and Cory's fiancée, Hannah, walked out. She was a beautiful girl with long shiny blond hair and blue eyes. She had a model figure, with long legs, and her silver dress was stunning.

Hannah sniffled and reached for a tissue. "It's fine. I just wish I could enjoy this party more. I recently found out that I'm almost three months pregnant, and I'm just sick all the time. I didn't know it would be like this."

Gina had never been pregnant, but she'd been around enough people to know that the morning sickness was usually the worst in the first trimester.

"I'm no expert, but I think it will probably ease up in another week or two."

"I hope so." Hannah tried to smile, but Gina could see it was a real effort. "I know we were introduced, but I'm terrible with names. I'm Hannah."

"I'm Gina."

"Thanks for trying to make me feel better. I'm going to see if I can fix my face before heading back out there." She pulled a tube of concealer and lipstick out of her purse.

"Hope you feel better, Hannah."

Gina headed back to the table, feeling sympathy for Hannah. She couldn't imagine being so young and getting pregnant and engaged so quickly. She hoped it would work out for them. It made her appreciate that she'd never rushed into a relationship and gotten so serious so fast. Sometimes she felt a little sad that she was still single when everyone around her seemed to be paired up or having kids, but she knew it was the right choice for her. She had faith that true love—kids and family— might still happen for her. She didn't generally focus on it, but suddenly, with two men that seemed interested, she'd been thinking about it more and trying to picture what her life would be like with each of them.

She liked Alex, but his world of flashy wealth and a sixty- to seventy-hour workweek was all-consuming. She remembered a conversation she'd had with Mandy once where she'd said one of the frustrations in her marriage was that Cory was so focused on appearances and that he had strongly discouraged her working. She could see that with Todd and Jim's relationships. Bethany and Jessica seemed happy not to work, but Gina knew she'd miss it.

She found herself missing Jared and wishing he was here to experience the Whitley. They would be laughing together at the ridiculousness of the Lawson Group's opulence. And she knew Jared would never suggest that she not work. She liked that they actually worked together and had similar hours. And she knew that eventually Jared would have his own restaurant.

But she also thought she was getting way ahead of herself. She'd only gone out with each of them a few times. And they were both nice guys.

When she sat back at the table, Todd was high-fiving Alex.

"Get the Porsche, man. You can afford it. Girls love Porsches. Don't they, Gina?"

"What?" Gina felt like she'd missed part of the conversation.

"I was just telling Todd that I was planning to get a car."

"Oh, and you want a Porsche? Those are nice." Gina had never been impressed with expensive cars. It always seemed like a waste of money to her. She supposed a Porsche was important to the guys for appearance's sake. There were a lot of luxury cars on Nantucket, so it would fit right in.

"Something like a Jeep might be more practical though. You could take it on the beach," she suggested.

"That's true," Alex said.

"Trust me, you don't want a Jeep. Go with the Porsche."

Alex grinned. "All right, Porsche it is."

Gina pictured Jared's Jeep. She felt much more comfortable in that. Or her Jetta, which was perfectly fine.

The night ended up going much later than Gina expected. It was a fun time though. There was a band that played a good mix of music, and they all danced after a fantastic dinner. Stacy and Gina visited the dessert station, helping themselves to chocolate mousse and cappuccino while the guys all went outside to smoke a cigar and drink cognac.

Finally, around midnight, Cory and Hannah said goodbye and that was the signal for everyone else to leave. Alex had a wonderful time bonding with his work colleagues. Gina could see him following in Todd and Jim's footsteps. He had their same enthusiasm and drive. She wondered about Stacy's husband, John, if he fit in as well. He was much quieter, but Alex said he was gifted with numbers, so she hoped he'd do well with the company too.

Alex stumbled a bit as they walked outside, and Gina was glad she'd been careful with what she drank. The valet went for her car and she drove them home. Alex was still on a high and chatted nonstop as they drove.

"Aren't those guys awesome? That's going to be me soon. A two-million-dollar bonus and a house right on the beach. And a Porsche! I can get the

Porsche now. I'll lease it. Sure, it'll be expensive, but it's worth it."

"That sounds nice, Alex." All the talk of money got boring after a while. It was all the guys seemed to talk about. Gina pulled into Alex's driveway.

"Well, thank you for inviting me. It was a fun party."

"It was!"

He leaned over to kiss her good night, and she turned her head at the smell of alcohol on his breath. His kiss landed on the side of her mouth, and he pulled back quickly. "Good night, Gina."

She waited until he was safely inside before driving off. It had been an interesting and eye-opening night. She'd gotten a much better sense of what Alex and his life would be like, and it was a world that she wasn't eager to be part of. He was a nice enough guy, but he wasn't the one for her.

16

On her way to work the next night, Gina found herself feeling both nervous and excited to see Jared. She felt a shift in her feelings toward him and hoped that he felt the same.

The restaurant was busy when she arrived. Mandy was at the front desk and showed her the reservations book before she headed to the bar. When she glanced at the bar, she saw that almost all of the seats were full, which was unusual for the time of day.

"Hey, Gina. Looks like it's going to stay busy tonight. Lunch was steady, and we're almost fully booked with reservations from five onward," Mandy said.

Jared stopped by once for sodas for him and Paul, but Gina was too busy to say more than hello. It wasn't until the end of the night over after-shift drinks that she had a chance to really talk to him.

He didn't ask her about what she'd done the night before, so she brought it up.

"I went to Alex's company Christmas party last night at the Whitley Hotel."

Jared's eyes clouded over. After a long moment, he spoke. "Fancy place. Was it a good time?"

"It was fun," she admitted and noticed a muscle in his jaw tense. "But, I won't be going out with Alex again."

"No?"

"He's a nice guy, but he's not for me. That world isn't for me. He's about to buy a Porsche. I drive a Jetta. I like my Jetta."

He smiled. "And I like my Jeep."

"It's a much more practical car for Nantucket," she agreed.

The others joined them at the bar—Gina, Billy, Emma and Paul, and a few of the waitresses. Billy had them all laughing as he usually did. About an hour or so later, when everyone was ready to go home, Jared walked her to her car.

"What are your plans for Christmas?" he asked.

"I don't really have any. Mandy told me I'm welcome to join them, but she has a houseful of people. I thought I'd just relax at home. Why?"

"Why don't you come to my house? It's only me and my mother, and I'm cooking. I'd love to cook for you too. It will be fun."

Gina was very tempted. "Are you sure she won't mind?"

"Yes, I'm sure. My mom will love you."

"Okay. I'll come. What can I bring?"

"Nothing. Well, maybe a bottle of wine if you want, something red."

"I can do that."

Gina picked up an extra shift, working Tuesday night, which was usually her night off, because they added a last-minute Christmas party. She didn't mind doing it. Customers generally were in a very good mood this time of year, and they were more generous than usual.

She finished up her shopping during the day and picked up a good bottle of wine to bring to Jared's mother's house. She also planned to pick up a bouquet of flowers for her, and she had something in mind for Jared. She'd stopped into Mitchell's Book Corner and was thrilled when she saw that they had signed copies of Dennis Lehane's newest release. She remembered that Jared had said he was a favorite author.

She was looking forward to working Christmas Eve. They would be closing early, at eight o'clock, and many of her regular customers had said they'd stop in either for a drink at the bar or for dinner too. She was planning to go to the nine o'clock Christmas Eve service, and she was secretly hoping for snow, just some light flurries. There was something magical about snow falling during the Christmas Eve service.

———

Christmas Eve was a busy day at Mimi's Place. They had reservations all day, with lots of people coming for early dinners so they could make church services. Mandy, Jill, and Billy were working the day shift, and Gina and Emma and Paul were on for the evening shift. They'd see Emma on Christmas Day though, since the restaurant was closed and Mandy was having everyone over.

Abby, Kate, and Kristen Hodges came in for lunch, and Mandy chatted with them a bit before they left. While she was visiting at their table, Connie Boyle walked by and joined her daughter at a table by the window. Mandy knew that Connie's daughter was in town for Christmas. Connie had told her how much she was looking forward to seeing her.

"You know," Abby said, once Connie was out of earshot, "I'm pretty sure that Connie anonymously donated money to the pantry so we can buy a new freezer."

"Really? Why do you think it's her?" Mandy asked, though it didn't surprise her. She knew that Connie had the means to make a sizable donation. Her second husband had left her quite well-off.

"She was one of the few people who knew that we needed a new freezer and what it would cost to replace it. And I think she's helped other people too. I've noticed that often soon after Connie hears about someone that needs help, help arrives. Sometimes it's money; sometimes it's helping in other ways by bringing people together."

Mandy thought of Connie suggesting that Cory's company might be a good place for Stacy's husband and asking Emma if there was room in the walk-in freezer. And the mysterious donation made to the young mother with the burst pipes.

"I suspect you may be right."

———

After Abby and her sisters left, Mandy stopped by Connie's table to say hello, and Connie introduced her to her daughter Miriam.

"She's my oldest and lives in Wellesley. My other daughter is out in California, and we see her every other Christmas."

They chatted for a bit, and Mandy said, "I heard the food pantry received a generous donation and now they can buy a new freezer."

Connie smiled. "Well, that's good news, isn't it?"

"It's a wonderful thing, whoever did it."

Connie was quiet and then said, "You know, many years ago when I was a young widow, I was struggling. My water heater had burst, and that took most of my savings. I had a choice to make:

pay my mortgage and have no Christmas presents, or pay it late. I really didn't want to pay it late because having good credit is so important. I told your grandmother I'd decided to pay the mortgage late because I couldn't imagine not having gifts for my girls and a nice holiday dinner. I received a bank check in the mail that week that covered my mortgage and left me with enough money to have a special Christmas. I knew it was your grandmother, though she never did admit it. She didn't want the credit; she just wanted to help as best she could."

Connie smiled. "That always stayed with me. I think it's a good way to be, if you're able to do it. Don't you think?"

Miriam reached out and squeezed her mother's hand. "You and Rose were quite a team for many years."

"We were, weren't we?" She looked up at Mandy. "You can't tell a soul. I'll deny it if you do. But your grandmother and I teamed up for many years after that. We had so much fun helping where we could and not just at Christmas. Just little things, nothing too outrageous. It made us feel good and useful. I still miss your grandmother," she admitted.

"I do too. Thank you, Connie, for all that you do, and Merry Christmas to both of you."

———

Mandy opened the oven and slid in the tray of mac and cheese that Paul had given her when she headed home on Christmas Eve. He'd made a little extra because he knew Brooke and Blake loved it, and Mandy had complained that they had no interest in eating what the rest of them would be having: lobster casserole and filet mignon. Soon she'd put the filets in to roast. The lobster was already cooked and tossed with butter, breadcrumbs, parsley, and a drizzle of good sherry. It just needed a few minutes in the oven to heat up. She knew Jill and Billy were looking forward to it—and she was too.

Jill and Billy were upstairs, showering and getting changed. The kids had been dropped off about an hour ago, but the house felt eerily quiet. She smiled to herself, suspecting where they might be. She walked into the living room and stood quietly, listening. And then she heard a soft whisper but couldn't make out the words.

"Brooke, Blake, are you two behind the tree? Come on out and hang your stockings. We'll be eating dinner soon." There was a shuffle and then laughter as the kids wiggled out from behind the Christmas tree.

"Here you go." Mandy handed each of them a stocking with their name embroidered at the top. They carefully hung them on heavy reindeer that were weighted to stay on the fireplace mantel and had hooks for the stockings. She'd picked up extra stockings earlier in the week for Jill and Billy and had the kids hang those as well. She added her own stocking, and they stood back and surveyed the mantel. It looked good and very festive. Jill had contributed earlier in the week by adding tiny lights along the top and a fragrant pine garland decorated with cranberries.

"Look, the ferry is coming in," Blake said.

They all looked out the big bay window in the living room that overlooked the ocean, and in the distance they could see the Steamship Authority high-speed ferry entering the harbor. Mandy knew that meant it was nearly six. Every day at the same time, they'd see the ferries come and then go fifteen minutes later. She never tired of the view.

"Something smells good."

Mandy turned at the sound of Billy's deep voice.

"It's our mac and cheese. Paul made it for us. But you can have some too, if you want," Blake said.

Billy laughed. "Well, that's nice of you. Thanks, buddy."

"You might want to hold off, Billy," Jill said. "You might prefer the rest of Mandy's menu. Lobster and steak."

Mandy smiled. "There's plenty of everything.

Let's go into the kitchen, and I'll put the appetizers out."

She put the filets in to roast, along with some red new potatoes and a tray of pigs in blankets, while Jill set out a platter of shrimp cocktail. Billy opened a bottle of Lion Tamer cabernet that he and Jill had brought with them for the occasion and poured a glass for each of them.

Mandy set out a dish of her favorite holiday dip, a white-bean hummus with garlic, lemon, and lots of parsley for color. She had chopped fresh vegetables and toasted pita bread for dipping.

The wine was rich and delicious, and they relaxed around the kitchen island. As soon as they were done, Mandy set out the tray of pigs in a blanket, the tiny cocktail franks wrapped in crescent dough that the kids had put together earlier. It was a holiday tradition that they loved to help with, and if it were up to them, they would have gobbled the whole tray down, but Mandy made them stop after a few so they wouldn't ruin their appetites for dinner.

When everything was ready, they ate in the dining room. It was all delicious, and they went back for second helpings of everything, including wine.

"I'm so glad that we decided to come for the whole month," Jill said as she reached for another small scoop of lobster.

"Yeah, Jill and I were just saying that upstairs while we were getting ready. It's been a nice break from the office and great to see you all. Especially these two monkeys." Billy grinned at Brooke and Blake, who adored having their new uncle around.

"I'm so glad you were able to come. It's been nice having a house full of people, of family." Mandy was grateful and was going to be sad to see them go. The house would miss their energy.

"What's Matt doing? Is he coming by later?" Jill asked.

"Not tonight. He's with his kids. They are home from college. He's going to stop over tomorrow night though."

Later, once dinner was all cleared up, the kids watched their favorite holiday movie, *Home Alone*. The rest of them enjoyed watching it too. When it finished, they headed to church for the nine o'clock Christmas Eve service. Mandy knew that flurries were in the forecast, and the kids were thrilled when it started to snow on their way to church. It put her in a good mood too, and she felt a swell of happiness to be surrounded by her favorite people on this special night. She missed Emma and Paul and most of all Matt, but she knew she'd be seeing them all soon.

17

"Do you mind working Christmas Eve? I feel a little guilty that we might be keeping you from something," Carol, one of Gina's favorite customers, asked. Carol and her husband, George, were eating dinner at the bar.

Gina smiled. "You're not keeping me from anything. I actually really like working Christmas Eve. It's not a late night. We close at eight, so I'll still be able to make it to the Christmas Eve service, and I hear we might get a little snow, which makes me very happy."

"Oh good. I heard that about the snow too. I think it's just supposed to be a dusting, which is perfect. Just enough for a white Christmas but not so much that it slows anything down."

"And hopefully no shoveling needed," George added.

Gina was steadily busy until they closed. She was feeling tired and happy because her customers, especially her regulars, had been very generous with their tips. The restaurant had emptied out since their last reservations were at seven. Most of the employees quickly left to get home to their families, but Emma, Paul, and Jared gathered in the bar for an after-work drink. They all wanted to try a glass of Gina's holiday cocktail, which was a mix of spices, fruit, champagne, and a splash of Grand Marnier orange liqueur. Gina poured one for herself too and sat next to Jared. She had just about enough time to enjoy one drink before walking a few streets over for the Christmas Eve church service.

"Gina, are you going to the nine o'clock service too?" Emma asked.

"Yes, I was planning on it."

"Good, we'll walk over with you. Mandy and the others will probably be there too."

"Maybe I'll join you all too. I was just going to go home, but it's still early, and I haven't been to a church service in too long," Jared said.

"It's hard when we usually work doubles on Sunday," Gina agreed.

Jared grinned. "That's one reason. I do well to get there on Christmas and Easter. Christmas is my favorite one."

"Me too," Gina agreed as she looked out the window and smiled. As she'd hoped, it was starting to flurry a bit.

"I'll tell you one thing I'm grateful for." Paul looked at Jared. "It's been great having you in the kitchen. I think we make a good team, and I hope you're liking it here. Because you can't leave." They all laughed. Jared looked pleased to hear it.

"Thanks. And I do like it here. It's a good fit for me, and I really like the people." He glanced at Gina and smiled.

They finished their drinks, and Gina put the empty glasses in the dishwasher before they headed out. The air temperature had dropped a lot since she was last out, and she shivered and pulled her scarf more snugly around her neck. The snow swirled around them as they walked. It was coming down harder and looked so pretty.

When they reached the church less than ten minutes later, there was a crowd gathered outside waiting to go in.

"Emma!" Gina heard a familiar voice call. It was Jill. She, Billy, Mandy, and the kids were standing by the door waving. Gina and the others made their way over to them and went inside together and took up a whole row. The service was lovely, and the Christmas carols had everyone smiling.

When the service ended, it was still snowing but not as heavily as it was earlier. There was about a half inch or so of snow on the ground. Just enough so that they could officially call it a white Christmas. Gina and Jared chatted briefly with Mandy and others, wishing everyone a Merry Christmas before heading back to the restaurant and their cars. They said goodbye to Emma and Paul before Jared walked Gina to her car.

It was dark out, but in the glow of the outside lights, she could see an impish look on Jared's face as he reached in his pocket and held something up.

"Look what I found. Mistletoe. You know what that means…" He smiled as he leaned toward her and gently touched his lips to hers. It was a sweet kiss, and she felt a thrill rush through her, unlike with Alex. But it was over too quickly.

"Merry Christmas, Gina."

She smiled, feeling nothing but joy. "Merry Christmas, Jared. I look forward to seeing you tomorrow."

"Me too. See you around noon."

Gina wasn't sure how dressy to go and changed outfits from jeans to slightly more dressy black pants, a pretty red cashmere sweater, and a delicate pearl necklace her mother gave her when Gina graduated from college. The day before, she'd picked up a bouquet of flowers for Jared's mother and a bottle of Bread & Butter cabernet. She also had Jared's gift and had wrapped it that morning in green paper and a shimmering red ribbon.

She gave Boots some attention before she left and made sure she had plenty of food. Once she was in the car, she punched Jared's address into her GPS, and it wasn't long before she pulled onto his street. At the end of the road, almost at the ocean's edge, she saw his driveway and turned onto it. It was long and winding, and she passed a small cottage first and guessed that was where Jared lived. He'd said his cottage was on his mother's property.

When she came around a corner and saw the

main house ahead, her jaw dropped. It was one of the nicest homes she'd seen on the island, and Nantucket had plenty of beautiful homes. This one was on a large lot and was a big all-white house with light-blue shutters and a farmer's porch that wrapped around to the front of the house.

She parked next to Jared's Jeep and a silver Mercedes sedan, gathered her things from the back seat, made her way to the front door, and rang the doorbell. A few moments later, the door opened, and a smiling woman with an elegant silver bob and a red cashmere sweater and black pants greeted her. They looked at each other's outfits and laughed.

"You must be Gina. Come in, dear. I'm Ellen."

Gina stepped inside and noticed two things immediately. The house was breathtaking, with soaring high ceilings and windows that gave the effect of being on the water. But the overall feeling was more cozy and warm than imposing. Soft white sofas and chairs had colorful knit throws over them in pretty ocean shades of blue and green.

"It's nice to meet you. Thank you for letting me join you both."

"I'm glad you could join us. Jared's in the kitchen, cooking up a storm."

Gina handed her the flowers and she smiled. "That's so nice of you. They're lovely. I'll put them in some water. Let's head into the kitchen."

Ellen led the way down a long, winding hall. When they reached the kitchen, Jared looked up from something he was stirring on the stove and smiled.

"Hey, there." He saw the bottle of wine. "You can set that on the counter. Or if you want, open it, and we'll have some with dinner."

"I'll get an opener." His mother opened a drawer and handed one to Gina.

Gina noticed a real fireplace with a roaring fire. It was two-sided so you could enjoy the fire in the kitchen and in the adjacent dining area, which also faced the ocean and had incredible views. It was a little windy out, and the waves were higher than usual, with frothy white tips.

"Tell me what you think of this…if you think it needs more salt." Jared passed her a small spoon of something brown and fragrant, some kind of meat in sauce.

She swallowed the bite and wanted to swoon. "What is that? It doesn't need anything. It's perfect."

Jared looked pleased to hear it. He gave his mom a taste too, and she gave him two thumbs up.

"It's osso buco. And I'm just stirring a risotto to have with it. It's almost ready. I figured we'd relax with some wine and cheese and crackers first."

His mother set a cheese tray with several different kinds of cheeses and crackers on the kitchen's island so they could help themselves while Jared finished up. Gina poured a glass of wine for each of them, and after his mother urged her to have some cheese, she spread a familiar-looking aged goat cheese on a cracker.

"Is that Humbolt Fog?" she asked.

"It is. I remember you said you like that one." It was her favorite cheese—firm like goat in the middle and runny like Brie on the edges. She'd mentioned it briefly to Jared a few weeks ago and was surprised that he remembered.

"How long have you lived on Nantucket, Gina?" his mother asked.

"Not that long. A little over a year."

"How do you like it so far? Do you think you might stay? A lot of people move here, but it's not for everyone."

"I did question if I'd made the right decision a few times after I moved here, during the winter months when it's so quiet. But now I love it. And after the crazy business of summer, I appreciate the peace now in the colder months."

"I couldn't agree more. We used to come here for summer vacations, and when Jared's father and I divorced about ten years ago, I kept the Nantucket house, but I didn't move here right away. I didn't think I'd want to be here year-round, but now I can't imagine living anywhere else."

Jared set a sizzling cast-iron skillet in the middle

of the island and warned them not to touch the pan. Six steaming oysters Rockefeller sat on a bed of salt rocks. Gina wasn't a fan of raw oysters, but she loved them prepared this way—with spinach, an anise-flavored cream sauce, and a sprinkle of seasoned breadcrumbs.

"Jared makes the best version of these that I've ever had," his mother said. "Honey, can you grab the hot sauce, please?"

A moment later Jared set a bottle of Hawthorne Hot next to the oysters, and his mother added a few drops to her oyster. Gina liked hot sauce, so she did the same and took a bite. The flavors were intense and so good. She knew the liqueur used that gave the slight licorice taste was Pernod, and there was the perfect amount in the oysters. She reached for a second one, added the hot sauce, and took a closer look at the label. Hawthorne Hot was one of the top-selling hot sauces in the country, and in the fine print, she noticed that it was made in Massachusetts. She glanced at Jared.

"Are you related to the makers of this sauce?" She figured it was a long shot, but the last name wasn't that common.

He nodded. "Dad started the business right out of college. He couldn't find a hot sauce that he liked, so he made one and the rest is history."

"I had no idea." She realized that Jared's family was wealthier than most, by far. Yet she'd had no idea. He wasn't at all showy about it, like Alex.

"I don't mention it, really. I think I got my love of food from my dad though."

His mother smiled. "He definitely did. Jared used to love to help me in the kitchen."

Jared plated up the osso buco and risotto for each of them, and they ate in the dining room, with the merrily glowing fireplace and soothing views of the ocean.

"Jared, this is so good." It was the first time Gina had experienced his cooking. She knew he was talented because she'd heard people rave about the dishes he made at the restaurant. But this was better than anything she'd had there. "When you do eventually open your own restaurant, people are going to love it."

"Thank you. I'm not in a hurry. I figure three more years or so working with Paul, and then I'll start to seriously think about doing something."

His mother looked slightly concerned. "Will you stay on Nantucket? Or are you thinking of somewhere around Boston?"

He put her mind at ease. "Definitely Nantucket. I have no interest in going to Boston. I think what I want to do will work here."

"I'm sure it will, and you know I'm happy to have you stay here. When you're ready, honey, I know your restaurant will be a big success."

"You two are good for my ego." Jared beamed at both of them. "Save room for dessert."

Gina helped Ellen clear the plates and tidy up in the kitchen. They decided to wait a bit on dessert, have some coffee and play cards first. Ellen got a pen and paper, and they had a blast playing the game Pitch for several hours until dessert sounded like a good idea, and Jared jumped up to get it. He returned a few minutes later with slices of rich chocolate cream pie in a buttery shortbread crust, with fresh whipped cream and shaved chocolate curls on top. They all cleaned their plates, then went into the living room and watched the classic Christmas movie *A Christmas Story* together.

"Gina has never seen this one. And even though I've seen it a million times with you, I still missed a trivia question on it."

"Oh? What was the question?"

"What was the name of the next-door neighbors whose dogs ate the turkey?"

His mother laughed. "The Bumpuses. Did you really miss that?"

"I really did."

"That's okay. I still love you," she joked.

They settled in to watch the movie, and when it finished, Jared's mother excused herself and said she was going to go lie down for a little while. Gina understood totally. It was tempting because she was so full herself and feeling lazy after sitting for the past few hours, so she nodded gratefully when Jared offered her another cup of coffee.

"If I don't see you again later, it was lovely to meet you," his mother said. "I'm so glad that Jared invited you over to share the day with us. And thank you again for the flowers."

Gina thanked her as well, and after his mother went upstairs, Jared said he'd be right back. He brought two fresh coffee cups and returned a moment later with a gift bag with her name on it. It was stuffed with tissue paper and tied with a silver ribbon.

"It's just something little. I saw it while I was shopping, and I thought of you."

"Oh. Hold on. I got you something too." Gina hopped up and returned a moment later with his gift and handed it to him. He looked surprised and pleased.

"You go first," Jared said.

Gina carefully pulled out the tissue paper, reached inside the bag, and pulled out a brush set. The new brushes she needed and hadn't gotten around to getting yet. There was also a selection of watercolor paints in gorgeous shades. She felt her eyes grow damp. It was such a thoughtful gift.

"Thank you. I really appreciate it. I need these."

He grinned. "I know. And I had a good guess that you probably had been too busy to get them."

"I can't wait to use them and to throw my old ones out." She laughed. "Okay, your turn."

Jared unwrapped his gift and opened the book and saw Dennis Lehane's signature.

"This is awesome, thank you. I haven't read this one yet. I've been meaning to get it." He stood up and held out his hand. "Let's take a walk. I'll give you the tour, and we can stretch our legs."

He led her around the downstairs rooms: through the more formal living room, by an office, and into the room he said was his favorite—a library with bookcases lining all the walls and several plush leather chairs strewn about the room, all facing the huge wall-to-ceiling windows that overlooked nothing but ocean. It was serene and beautiful and cozy at the same time.

"It would be easy to spend hours in this room," Gina said.

"I have. Many times over the years. Come over here and see this view."

Gina walked to where Jared stood by the window.

He took her hand and looked serious for a moment. "I'm really glad that you came today. There's no one I'd rather spend the day with. I love spending time with you."

"I feel the same way. I always have fun and just love being with you too."

"Look up."

She did and laughed. There was a sprig of mistletoe taped to the window.

He laughed. "Smooth, huh? I thought you'd like that."

"I do. Very much."

He kissed her then, and this time it wasn't a short kiss.

18

The children were up early on Christmas Day—
which meant that Mandy was up early too. But she
didn't mind. The excitement of her children was
contagious, and she loved to feel the magic of the
day through their eyes. She'd been up late the night
before, finishing up her wrapping and chatting
with Jill and Billy. Their time with her had gone so
quickly, and they only had one more week together
before they headed home to Manhattan on New
Year's Day. They wanted to be on Nantucket for
New Year's Eve and home the next evening to go
into the office and see the team on Tuesday.

Jill and Billy heard the commotion, and Mandy could hear them getting up too. She went downstairs to the kitchen first to start the coffee, then into the living room, where the kids were sitting on the floor holding their overstuffed stockings. Mandy got the other stockings down and handed them to Jill and Billy when they joined them.

"Okay, you can go ahead and look inside now," Mandy told the kids. She'd had fun with their stockings, filling them with a mix of things they needed, like socks and underwear, and stuff they liked—candy, small toys, and books they'd requested. She and Jill had stuffed each other's stockings with their favorite things. She'd gotten a bag of York Peppermint Patties for Jill and Reese's Minis for Billy, and they'd gotten her a bag of gummy bears. Mandy had gotten them both soft, fuzzy socks and wasn't surprised to find a pair from them as well. Jill knew how she loved her warm socks.

When the stockings were emptied. Mandy told

the kids to wait one moment and went and got coffee for Jill, Billy, and herself.

"Okay, now you can open your gifts." The adults gratefully sipped their coffee and watched the kids open their presents. Mandy went around and scooped up the piles of wrapping paper and ribbons and stuffed everything in a giant trash bag. Once the kids had opened all of their gifts and were playing with a new game she'd given Blake, Mandy, Jill, and Billy exchanged gifts. They'd agreed to just do something small because none of them needed a thing.

Mandy had bought cashmere sweaters for both of them, rose pink for Jill and hunter green for Billy. She also gave each of them a book, the newest Danielle Steel for Jill and a Lee Child mystery for Billy.

Mandy opened her gift bag from Jill and Billy and noticed that they were both trying not to laugh.

"What is it?"

"You'll see," Jill said. Mandy smiled when she

unwrapped the first gift. It was an identical cashmere sweater to the one she'd given Jill, but a different color, pale lavender. It wasn't the first time they'd given each other the same gift.

"Great minds," Jill said. They'd been shopping together and had both admired the sweaters. Their other gift to her was a gorgeous framed print of one of Kristen Hodges's seaside paintings. Jill knew that Mandy liked Kristen's work because she had an original watercolor in the living room.

"I thought you might like that for your bedroom or maybe your office?"

"I love it, thank you."

Mandy put out the traditional Christmas morning coffee cake, cinnamon walnut by the Boston Coffee Cake company. Mandy had never even tried to make coffee cake because this one was so good, and it wouldn't be Christmas at her house without it.

They spent the morning relaxing, while the kids played with their new games.

Around eleven thirty, Jill and Mandy went to work in the kitchen. Jill peeled potatoes while Mandy made a garlic mixture to rub all over the prime rib before putting it in the oven to roast. They also had leftover lobster casserole and shrimp cocktail from the night before, and she was going to make a big salad. Billy wandered in and offered to help, but Jill shooed him away and suggested he see what was on for Christmas movies and they'd be in shortly to join him.

It didn't take them long in the kitchen, and they settled on the sofa with Billy just as the movie *It's a Wonderful Life* began.

Two hours or so later, there was a knock on the door, just as the movie was ending.

Mandy got up and opened the front door. Emma and Paul came in, with cheeks rosy from the cold and holding bags of gifts. Emma stopped short when she saw Mandy's damp eyes.

"Is everything all right?"

Mandy nodded and smiled. "Clarence just got his wings."

Emma laughed. "Of course."

The kids came running when they heard Emma's voice, and hugs were exchanged all around, followed by more gifts. Mandy had gotten Emma and Paul both comfy flannel pajamas. Emma loved pajamas. And books for both of them—the newest Nora Roberts suspense for Emma and a John Grisham legal thriller for Paul. Jill gave them a wine rack for their kitchen and a few bottles of really good wine. Emma and Paul gave each of them a luxurious plush bathrobe and fuzzy slippers, which Mandy and Jill both had recently said they needed.

Emma opened one of the bottles of wine, a cabernet, and let it breathe for a little bit, until they were ready to eat. They had it with their meal, and it was silky and rich, deliciously complementing the garlicky prime rib.

Jill raised a glass to toast everyone. "To being together. This past month has been wonderful." She looked at Billy. "I know you told your mom we'd come next Christmas, but we might need to find a way to do both. It was really special being here for December and working in the restaurant. It made me feel more a part of it, and I'm really proud of what you all have done with Mimi's Place."

"Thank you, and I'd love to see this be a new tradition too, having you both come for the month of December. I'm so glad that you did."

"Me too. It's been fun working with you both and just spending time with you. Paul and I were recently saying that we need to plan a trip to New York soon too."

"I'd love that. We have plenty of room, so you'll stay with us. And we'll show you all around and maybe see a show or two."

After they finished eating, Paul put out an apple pie he'd made that morning, and they had that for dessert before collapsing in the living room to relax and watch more Christmas movies.

A few hours later, Matt came by. His kids were home, so he didn't want to stay long, but he did want to see Mandy alone for a moment before they went to visit with the others.

"I have something for you. Can we go somewhere private where it's just the two of us?"

"Of course. I have something for you too." He waved at everyone as she led him into her office and closed the door. It was a small room, but she loved it. She often sat in one of the comfy plush chairs, read a book, and enjoyed the ocean view. Today it was cold and gray outside, and she thought she saw a hint of flakes starting again.

She handed him his gift bag and said he should go first. He smiled when he pulled out the coffee table book on fishing that she and Jill had found.

"This is great, thank you."

"There's something else in there."

He reached in and pulled out the sweater she'd chosen for him. She'd thought of him instantly when she'd seen it in the store. It was sturdy but soft and the color, a deep teal, was flattering on him.

"I love it. Thank you."

"If you want to exchange it, there's a gift receipt in the bag."

He smiled. "I don't need to exchange it. Now open yours." He handed her a very small box.

She unwrapped it carefully and was stunned to see a breathtakingly gorgeous ring inside. It was a sapphire, surrounded by tiny diamonds on a platinum band. It was beautiful and a much bigger gift than what she'd given him.

"This is lovely, but it's too much. You shouldn't have."

"I wanted to. I consulted my kids about this. I know you're nowhere near ready to think about getting married again. So, this is a promise ring. I wanted you to know how serious I am. You're it for me, Mandy. I'm in no rush, but when you're ready for an engagement ring, just let me know. Until then, I wanted you to know how much you mean to me. I hope you like it."

She felt her eyes grow damp again. "I love it. I really do. It's so generous of you. And I'm very serious about you too. I told my sisters a while back that there's no one else I want to date. Just you."

He looked relieved and smiled. "Good, because I think I love you, Mandy Lawson."

She felt filled with joy for the second time that day. "I know I love you too, Matt."

He pulled her into his arms and showed her how he felt. She loved kissing Matt, but when he reluctantly pulled apart, she agreed they should probably go join the others.

"Merry Christmas, Mandy," he said softly.

She looked up at him and into the kind, handsome eyes that reflected the happiness she felt.

"Merry Christmas, Matt."

19

It was Jill's suggestion to have a private New Year's Eve party for staff and friends once the restaurant closed for the night. They knew they wanted to do something fun for New Year's Eve, but they were also all working, so it made things easier to just stay at Mimi's Place and celebrate there. The last customer left a little after ten, and they locked the doors and turned up the music. Paul set out some appetizers and sandwiches in case anyone was hungry, and Gina poured drinks for everyone.

Jill noticed that Jared and Gina seemed to be an item now. The two of them had been inseparable since Christmas and seemed to be head over heels for each other.

And she was thrilled to see Mandy so happy with Matt. He'd arrived shortly before they closed. She and Emma had met at the Corner Table for lunch a few days ago, and both agreed that they no longer thought Mandy needed to date anyone else. Matt seemed crazy about her, and the sapphire ring he gave her for Christmas spoke volumes. He'd told Mandy he was ready to get engaged whenever she was, and Jill didn't doubt it. She knew Mandy wasn't in a rush for that though, and that Matt understood.

"Penny for your thoughts," Billy said.

She smiled up at him. They were sitting at the bar sipping Gina's New Year's Eve punch. Jill wasn't sure what was in it, but it was delicious.

"I was just thinking how glad I am that we decided to do this. It was good for Mandy and for us. It's been fun working in the restaurant."

"It has been. If this recruiting thing doesn't work

out, I know I could always get a job in a restaurant now. Mandy said I'm a natural."

She laughed. He really was though. He knew most of the regular customers by name now, and he made everyone feel welcome and special. It was a simple thing, but people loved to feel appreciated, and it kept them coming back.

"I'm so glad we came to our senses and found each other," he said. They'd been best friends and business partners for so many years. It wasn't until Jill spent a year working on Nantucket that they both realized that their friendship had deepened into the kind of love that lasts.

"Me too. And since we've been married, it's only gotten better. I really do want to do this again next year. Do you?"

He nodded. "We'll find a way to make it work. Maybe we can come here right before Thanksgiving next year and fly home on Christmas Eve day."

Jill nodded. "That sounds good, and then the year after, we get Christmas here again. I have something else I want to tell you. I think it will make you really happy." It was something she'd been thinking about more and more, ever since the Hodgeses' open house.

"What's that?"

"I think I might be ready to start trying."

"Are you serious? That's fantastic. Are you sure?" Billy looked like he'd won the lottery.

"I'm sure. But I don't want to say anything yet, in case it doesn't happen right away."

"Whatever you want. Thank you." He leaned over and showed her how much he appreciated her with a quick kiss. And then whispered in her ear that he loved her.

"What are you two plotting?" Emma asked as she and Paul walked over. Mandy and Matt were right behind them.

"World domination," Billy joked.

"Christmas plans for next year. We're definitely coming again for a month, but we might come for Thanksgiving instead and leave just before Christmas, if that works for Mandy, of course."

Mandy smiled. "Thanksgiving could be fun. Whatever works for you two is fine by me. As long as you come."

Jill lifted her glass. "To a Happy New Year for everyone and to next year at Mimi's Place."

Jared and Gina wandered over arm in arm and joined the toast, lifting their glasses high. "To Mimi's Place!"

"And family and good friends," Mandy added.

"Always." Emma clicked her glass against her sisters'. "Happy New Year!"

Thank you so much for reading. I hope you enjoyed *Christmas at the Nantucket Restaurant.*

If you'd like to be notified when I have a new release, or other good news, visit my website, pamelakelley.com, to sign up for an email notification.

You are also invited to join my Pamela Kelley Reader Group on Facebook. It's a friendly bunch of avid readers, and we do fun things, have occasional exclusive giveaways, and I often ask for input on new covers, character names, book titles, etc.

READ ON FOR MORE
FROM PAMELA KELLEY IN
THE NANTUCKET RESTAURANT.

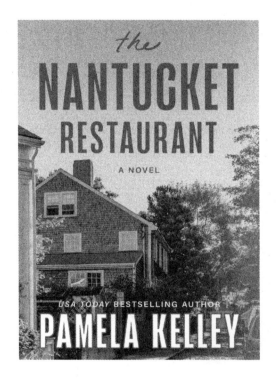

NOW AVAILABLE FROM
SOURCEBOOKS LANDMARK.

1

Jill O'Toole wasn't supposed to be surfing the net on a busy Thursday afternoon. Her to-do list was a mile long, and the most pressing item was front and center on her desk. A crisp three-page Excel spreadsheet of candidate research, which her assistant had printed out, highlighted, paper-clipped, and delivered to her an hour ago. Names and numbers of people she needed to call ASAP.

Instead, she was mesmerized by a food blog, which was one of her guilty pleasures. It featured mouthwatering photos, recipes, and related stories that made her long to be home puttering around her own kitchen, slicing and dicing, stirring and tasting. No time to browse today however, for she was on a mission to find a foolproof recipe for the kind of rich, dense, fudgy chocolate cake that would inspire moans at first bite.

Jill could almost always tell just by reading the recipe what a dish would taste like, and she knew that the one she'd just found was as close to the signature dessert at Mimi's Place as she was going to get. Hopefully, Grams would agree.

For as long as she could remember, they'd always gone to Mimi's Place for Grams's birthday. An elegant two story restaurant that was walking distance from Grams's Nantucket home, Mimi's Place served Italian-influenced meals that were simple yet exquisite comfort food. Certain dishes, such as their wafer-thin eggplant parmesan, were so amazing that Jill finally gave up ordering them anywhere else.

Usually, these birthdays consisted of just the immediate family—Jill and her sisters, Emma and Mandy. Mandy's husband, Cory, and their two young children, Blake and Brooke, were always there too, since they lived on Nantucket. But Emma's husband, Peter, usually stayed home in Phoenix. He barely knew Grams, and it was just so far to come. Emma and Peter had separated two months ago. And Emma hadn't said why, only that she'd fill Jill and Mandy in when she saw them.

Jill and her sisters had always been close to Grams, but even more so since their mother passed away almost twelve years ago after an unexpected and short battle with pancreatic cancer. Their father had followed six months later. The doctors called it a massive coronary; Grams said it was simply a broken heart.

Last year, when Grams turned ninety, they threw a real party at Mimi's Place. Grams had always been a social butterfly, eating out once, if not twice a day, because she couldn't justify cooking for one. All her friends who were still living and able to make it came, along with what seemed like most of Nantucket. Everyone knew and loved Grams and wanted to celebrate her. They filled the entire restaurant, and it was quite a party. This year, however, would be different. Grams had decided about nine months ago that it was time to downsize. Her house, just off Nantucket's Main Street, where she'd lived for over fifty years, was too big.

"As much as I hate to admit it, the stairs are killing me, and I don't have the energy to start renovating now. I'm going to move into the assisted living at Dover Falls."

Still determined and feisty at barely five feet tall and maybe ninety-five pounds, Grams had smiled brightly and added, "Connie Boyle is there. She goes to Foxwoods Casino once a quarter. There's a whole busload that goes. Doesn't that sound fun?"

A month after making her announcement, it was a done deal. Grams sold two other properties that she'd owned for many years and rented out to summer tourists. She wasn't ready to part with her main residence though, or even to rent it out just yet.

Grams settled in quickly at Dover Falls and

always sounded happy whenever Jill or one of her sisters called, but recently she'd admitted to feeling a bit under the weather. A nasty bout of bronchitis had turned into pneumonia and left her so weak that she didn't have the strength to venture out at all, let alone make the traditional trip to Mimi's Place. Grams's suite at Dover Falls had a small kitchen they could use, so the new plan was for Jill to make the cake ahead of time and then just see what everyone was in the mood for when they all arrived.

Jill was mentally making a shopping list of the ingredients she'd need when an instant message from her assistant flashed on the computer screen.

> Billy's on his way in. I told him you
> were busy, but he wouldn't listen. Just
> wanted to give you a heads-up.

Thank God for Jenna. She was the best assistant Jill had ever had, and she couldn't imagine working without her.

"I knew you weren't on the phone," Billy said, barging into the office and sitting on the edge of her desk. He picked up the spreadsheet of names. "Have you even called any of these candidates yet? You know how important this search is?"

Jill sighed. Her partner, Billy Carmenetti, was prone to drama. He wore expensive suits, drove a shiny new BMW, and had house accounts at several of the hottest restaurants. If you didn't know him better, you'd think Billy wanted people to think he was someone important. But Jill did know better. She knew that he just liked nice things because he'd grown up without them. At six foot two, with thick, almost black hair, dark brown eyes that perpetually danced with mischief, and a long, lean body, toned from daily gym workouts, Billy was hard to miss.

He was also one of the most generous people she knew and one of the nicest, even if he did drive her crazy on a daily basis. They'd been best friends and business partners for well over a decade, and it was only a month ago Jill realized that she might be in love with him. The idea had slammed into her, fully formed and obvious, and she was struggling with what to do about it.

"I know, I know. I'm about to dive into it. I just had something important I had to handle first."

Billy turned as the printer whirred and groaned. Curious, he leaned over and plucked the freshly printed page from the tray. He glanced at it, then raised his eyebrows at Jill. "Chocolate cake? Are you kidding me?"

"Oh, relax. It's for Grams's birthday. I'm on this search. Don't worry. We'll fill it."

"We have to. If we don't, we won't get the rest of their business. I heard from their CFO that they are using this search as a test to see how we do and what caliber of candidates we can produce. If we get into this company, it could launch us to the next level. Continued business for years to come."

"Don't you have somewhere you need to be, other searches of your own to worry about?" Jill teased.

"I'm going, I'm going." He swung his legs off her

desk and headed toward the door. He turned back and smiled, his voice softer this time. "Tell Grams I said happy birthday."

And that was one of the many reasons why she loved Billy. He adored her grandmother. More importantly though, he was just a good person, through and through. And they were as close if not closer than most married couples. Everyone said so and constantly asked why they weren't a couple. They'd always laughed it off and said it was impossible as they'd been friends forever. They were like brother and sister as well as business partners. So the realization that she might be in love with him was troubling. Especially when she considered that Billy had never given the slightest inkling that he was even remotely attracted to her.

ACKNOWLEDGMENTS

Thank you to my early readers, Jane Barbagallo, Taylor Hall, Cindy Tahse, and Amy Petrowich. And to my editors at Sourcebooks/Landmark, Deb Werksman, Diane Dannenfeldt, and Aimee Alker; to Cristina Arreola in marketing; and Heather VenHuizen for this gorgeous cover design. Thank you also to Dominique Raccah for believing in these books.

ABOUT THE AUTHOR

Pamela Kelley is a *USA Today* and *Wall Street Journal* bestselling author of women's fiction, family sagas, and suspense. Her books are often described as feel-good reads with people you'd want as friends.

She lives in a historic seaside town near Cape Cod and just south of Boston. She has always been an avid reader of women's fiction, romance, mysteries, thrillers, and cookbooks. She's an avowed foodie and loved creating a novel set in a restaurant where so many scenes could be infused with delicious food.